P9-EMF-274

JAN HAMBRIGHT

ON FIRE

HARLEQUIN®

TORONTO • NEW YORK • LONDON
AMSTERDAM • PARIS • SYDNEY • HAMBURG
STOCKHOLM • ATHENS • TOKYO • MILAN • MADRID
PRAGUE • WARSAW • BUDAPEST • AUCKLAND

To the men and women who answer the page every day
at great risk to their own safety. Thank you.

To Peggy, Janis and Lynn, the brainstorm babes.
Thank you.

For my mom and Grandma. Wish you were here,
but I know you're stuck in heaven.

ISBN-13: 978-0-373-22943-7
ISBN-10:   0-373-22943-7

ON FIRE

Copyright: © 2006 by M. Jan Hambright

www.eHarlequin.com

Printed in U.S.A.

ABOUT THE AUTHOR

Jan Hambright penned her first novel at seventeen, but claims it was pure rubbish. However, it did open the door on her love for storytelling. Born in Idaho, she resides there with her husband, three of their five children, a three-legged watchdog and a spoiled horse named Texas, who always has time to listen to her next story idea while they gallop along.

A self-described adrenaline junkie, Jan spent ten years as a volunteer EMT in rural Idaho, and jumped out of an airplane at ten thousand feet, attached to a man with a parachute, just to celebrate turning forty. Now she hopes to make your adrenaline level rise along with that of her danger-seeking characters. She would like to hear from her readers and hopes you enjoy the story world she has created for you. Jan can be reached at P.O. Box 2537, McCall, Idaho 83638.

Books by Jan Hambright

HARLEQUIN INTRIGUE

865—RELENTLESS
943—ON FIRE

CAST OF CHARACTERS

Kade Decker—An ex-fireman turned arson investigator, he barely survived a fire that killed the victim he was trying to rescue. Now back home in Montgomery, Alabama, he's faced with a revenge arsonist's rampage.

Savannah Dawson—Being psychic has always felt like a curse. But when a recurring nightmare drives her to one arson fire after another, she becomes Kade Decker's prime suspect. Can she use her abilities to help him solve the crime?

Nick Brandt—Montgomery Police Department's lead detective, and Kade's college buddy.

George Welte—One of psychologist Savannah Dawson's patients, his obsessive, pyro-personality seems highly suspicious.

Shane Murphy—He likes to watch. Likes to videotape the fires. But is it a crime?

Todd Coleman—Kade's new next-door neighbor has always wanted to join the fire department.

Incident Commander Fisk—An old friend of Kade's father, a Montgomery fireman before he died doing what he loved. Fisk is at every fire scene, giving the knock-down orders and keeping an eye on Kade.

Don Watson—A savvy forensic technician, and the man with the answers.

Chapter One

Flames raged at the sky, reaching for the stars above, hazing them in a veil of thick black smoke.

Kade Decker trained his camera lens on the crowd behind a strip of yellow crime-scene tape, and clicked off a couple of shots.

He pulled back from the viewfinder and turned to watch the fire devour the vacant house, consuming the last of its corpse like a hungry animal, out of control.

Fire department practice burns drew pyromaniacs; he just hoped theirs decided to make an appearance tonight. He'd made sure the department publicized the information, hoping to capture an image he could use in his investigation.

Steam billowed into the air as the fire crew opened the valves on their hoses, turning water loose on the flames and ending their fiery feast.

He turned back to the crowd, which had begun to disperse, feeling some of their disappointment as they disappeared into the darkness one by one, their excitement put out along with the fire.

Raising the camera, he stared through the viewfinder and adjusted the focus.

The woman whose image he dialed in stood on the fringe of the scene, dressed in a long white gown.

Kade squeezed off a shot and lowered the camera, intrigued by her presence, dressed like an angel at such a hellish event.

"Hey, Decker."

"Yeah." He turned toward the fire chief.

"You get what you needed?"

"Let's hope. This blaze drew some strange ones. Maybe we caught an image of our guy. We'll compare these pictures with the police department videos. Maybe we'll get lucky."

"Hope so." The chief nodded and walked away.

Kade turned around, determined to speak to the woman. He scanned the remains of the crowd, but she was gone.

Disappointment rattled through him as he let the camera drop and hang from the strap around his neck. Squeezing the handle of his cane, he limped toward his car, anxious to get the pictures down to the station.

The Montgomery arsonist was still out there, burning, and he had to be stopped before someone died.

"BRING HER IN for questioning." Kade leveled his gaze on Nick Brandt, Montgomery's lead detective and his old college roommate. Tension wound around his nerves. He needed this job like he needed the air in the room.

"Do you want my expertise?"

"I won't BS you, we need your help. The department is shorthanded. This heat wave is stretching services thin and the arson fires have everyone on edge."

Kade refocused on the paused frame of video, studying the woman silhouetted against a wall of flame.

The woman in white…the same woman he'd taken photos of at the practice burn two nights ago. "Who is she?"

"Doctor Savannah Dawson. A local psychologist. The department has used her on some tough cases. She has a knack for finding the truth."

"She works the mental angle?"

"You could say that."

He didn't like the embarrassed grin on Nick's face or the feeling there was more to the story than he was willing or able to share.

"We did a background check going back ten years. She grew up in Atlanta, moved here five years ago. She's a model citizen, well respected…"

"Beautiful." Kade finished the sentence and felt a jolt of irritation rattle his nerves. "She's a looker, but that's not a perquisite for exclusion. How do you explain her presence in four pieces of department footage taken at the arson scenes, and again at the practice burn?"

"I can't."

"Then let me do my job. If she's innocent, she'll walk out of here. Take the first round of interrogation if it makes you feel better. I'll watch, see what I can pick up."

His friend straightened and he tapped him on the shoulder. "What's the problem? You have a hot date with her, and handcuffs don't go with your dinner jacket?"

Nick smirked. "Nah."

"Too bad." He watched his buddy leave the room and turned back to the TV screen. Pulling his tie loose from his shirt collar, he peeled the top button out of its loop, letting some heat out.

July in Montgomery was a scorcher and the heat wave showed no sign of letting up, but neither was the arsonist who'd set three fires in a week. Same MO, same general area.

The woman caught on video hovering nearby at every scene was a break he couldn't afford to ignore. It was textbook, he could feel it in his bones. Arsonists enjoyed babysitting their creations. Was she any different? He'd have her confession before the day closed, then he could wrap things up. Put a notch in his belt, prove he was capable, again, and not just coasting on his father's good name.

He picked up the TV remote, but couldn't kill the image. He studied her face, framed in waves of long, dark hair. She had a heart-shaped face and full lips.

Slight, willowy build. Hell, she looked like an angel, in a devilish sort of way. He couldn't see the color of her eyes, but he could almost imagine they were a heavenly shade of blue, though he didn't know where the thought came from.

Moving up to the screen, he focused on her choice of clothing. It was the same nightgown, just like the one she'd been wearing when he captured her on film. He'd never spotted an arsonist in their pajamas, hanging out at the scene of the crime looking like some sort of guardian angel. It was a heck of an odd MO.

He pushed the button and she vanished.

Female arsonists were a rarity, but they did come along every now and again. He picked up his cane and briefcase, a small measure of excitement tumbling in his gut.

This was his first case. His first shot at a comeback. He couldn't afford to blow it. Besides, the only good pyro was an extinguished pyro, even if catching him took second place to actually putting out the flames.

If they didn't get you first.

He leaned on his cane, gritted his teeth and left the room, striding along the corridor to Interrogation, with its two-way mirror and closed in walls.

Pain radiated in his hip, putting a hitch in his step. He paused and opened the door into the tiny watch room.

It had been ten months since the accident. Twenty-eight weeks of grueling physical therapy, and still the pain was excruciating. It sawed into him every time he moved, but it wouldn't break him; he wasn't going to let it.

Nothing was going to stop him from doing this job.

Not even a sizzling pyro in her nightgown.

SAVANNAH DAWSON tried to relax in the hard plastic chair and focused her attention on the officer sitting across the table from her.

She'd met him briefly a couple of times in the course of working a case, but today was different; she could feel it in the air around her.

Nervous energy jumped and bumped along her spine, but she held direct eye contact, a slight smile on her lips. She even resisted the overwhelming urge to glance at her watch. Her ten o'clock appointment would be walking into the clinic right now, and the sooner she took care of this the better.

"What's this about, Detective Brandt? Has there been some sort of accident? Do you have one of my patients in lockup, needing evaluation?"

"No, no. Nothing like that, but I would like to know where you were last night, between midnight and 2:00 a.m.?"

"Sleeping." She shifted under his intense gaze, hoping her answer hadn't sounded curt.

"There was another arson fire last night. A residence on Catalpa Street. We took video, and you're in it. Want to tell me what you were doing there?"

"But, I wasn't there. I was at home, in bed. There must be some mistake." Caution inched along her nerves. She didn't need a map to see where he was trying to take her. "Did you speak to me personally?"

"No."

"There you have it. I'm not the only brunette in Montgomery."

"I've seen the video. It's you."

"I went to bed around 10:00 p.m. last night, and woke up this morning at six. It's crazy to think I could have been there without knowing or remembering."

He nodded, a fixed smile on his lips. "You're right. And you'd know crazy if you came across it. Would you like to see the video?"

"I'll take a look. Maybe I can help you decipher who she is."

Nick Brandt stood up. "It's an open investigation, Doctor Dawson. We need to follow every lead and nail this firebug before he hurts someone."

"I understand. Forget it. They say everyone has a twin somewhere in the world. Maybe mine just happens to live in Montgomery." She stood up and gathered her handbag, her gaze drifting to a large mirrored wall in the room. It looked like something straight out of an episode of *Law & Order,* but the vibes coming from the other side were real.

Someone was watching her.

She could feel him behind the glass, knew their exchange of words was being scrutinized, dissected and worse. Disbelieved?

"It's down the hall in the video room."

She fell in behind the detective, the weight of the observer's thoughts trailing along with her. She resisted the urge to shake them off. It wouldn't do any good; they'd only come back, and stronger next time.

Her psychic gift was expanding, shifting, had been for the last three weeks, but she didn't want to know the feelings and emotions of others. She didn't enjoy picking up on information that didn't belong to her, or in her head, for that matter.

Then there was the recurring nightmare…

"The video was taken last night around 1:00 a.m."

She followed him into a small, windowless room with minimal furniture and aged blue carpet.

He picked up a remote and turned on the television in the corner. "The fire is similar to two others. All of them were set using the same MO."

A paused video clip popped on screen.

She blinked hard, trying to reconcile the image and the sick feeling tossing around in her stomach. "It's me…but I don't understand…"

He was coming…the hunter was coming. Moving in on her like a lion on a kill. The man she'd felt X-ray her soul. Had he discovered her secret?

Her palms became slick, her heartbeat intensified until it throbbed in her eardrums.

"Doc? Are you all right?"

"It's so hot in here." She pulled at the front of her blouse, sending little puffs of air against her inflamed skin.

"The AC's on the fritz. Sorry. Can I get you some water?"

"That would be nice. Thanks."

He left the room, but nothing was going to extinguish the growing heat in her body. She closed her eyes, her back to the open door. She didn't have to see the man to know he was there.

Like a frame of film in her head, she recorded the exact instant he appeared, standing in the doorway, his shoulder against the jamb, appraising her with an electric gaze that zapped her. She went weak in the knees, but regained her composure.

"Doctor Savannah Dawson, I presume?" His voice was deep and smooth.

She sucked in a breath, gathered her courage and turned around. "Yes."

Her mental picture of his face matched the physical one she found herself staring at now. Every detail was seared into her brain. His angular face, straight nose, almost black hair, cut short, and his eyes, an intense shade of hazel flecked with gold.

It was the face of the man she'd seen over and over…in her nightmare.

"Kade Decker, Montgomery's newest arson investigator. Just in from Chicago." He extended his right hand while he moved toward her.

In slow motion she reached out, intent on holding her ground. He may rule her nights, but this was daylight.

Their hands locked for an instant. Skin on skin.

A current of electricity shot up her arm and sizzled through her body.

Jerking free of his grip, she pinned a smile on her lips, but she knew he'd felt it to. She'd seen it in the brief widening of his eyes, a look of shock smoothed over.

"Pleased to meet you, Mr. Decker."

"Call me Kade."

"Okay." She couldn't do it any longer. She couldn't stand toe-to-toe with him, not when he seemed to suck the energy out of her body, leaving her feeling like a rag doll. She sank into the chair next to the desk.

What was it about him? What connection could they possibly share?

"Detective Brandt showed you the video. Can you explain it?"

She dragged her gaze away from his face and looked at the television screen.

"It's me. As for an explanation for how and why I'm there, I don't have one. I don't remember leaving the house last night, much less warming myself next to a fire without a roasting skewer and a bag of marshmallows."

A smile tugged at his mouth, and she felt him mentally fight it. Humor as a weapon could work. Disarm? She doubted it. He was too intense, after one thing. The truth.

"Do you sleepwalk, Savannah?"

The question was silly, but the use of her name in his easy Southern drawl sent small shivers through her body. "No."

"So how do you explain your presence at the scene? I have additional tapes with you on each and every one. Video doesn't lie."

He began to pace back and forth in front of the desk, each step accentuated by a slight hesitation before the next step followed. He'd been injured, somehow. She focused, picking up on a measure of the pain inside his body.

She got up from the chair, feeling less vulnerable to his power in a standing position. "If I had an explanation for being there, I'd share it with you, but I don't."

He pulled up short and turned on her.

She watched him clench his teeth, then relax, saw the minute beads of perspiration dotting his upper lip. A wisp of desire zinged through her, throwing her thoughts into a jumble. But were they her thoughts? Or his?

The desk offered a physical barrier between them, but she couldn't shut out his mental chatter. She could feel his determination churning like an unrelenting sea against the rocks. Or was it desperation?

"You think I set those fires, don't you?"

His gaze locked on to hers, warning, searching, penetrating. Her heart skipped a beat, and the air in the room thickened.

"You're free to leave, Dr. Dawson, but there'll be more questions, and a search warrant."

Fear tickled along her spine. She raised her chin in defiance. "You can search until they hand out ice picks in hell. It won't change a thing. I'm no arsonist."

"Then you don't have anything to worry about, do you? But if you're lying, I won't stop until I put you away."

She could only stare at him from across the desk, feeling his certainty about her guilt. The sensation was crushing, powerful. Her emotions imploded.

"I'll call my attorney." She straightened and walked to the door with as much moxie as she could manage.

Detective Brandt showed up with a glass of water and a frown on his face.

She sidestepped him and moved into the hall, taking a couple of strides, but the men's conversation radiated through the open doorway.

"What did you say to her, Decker?"

"Nothing really. She's in a hurry, her ten o'clock is waiting."

Savannah stopped short. Fear laced through her veins, but turned to curiosity. She hadn't told him about her ten o'clock patient. Could the psychic connection she'd felt between them really work both ways?

She took off at a brisk walk, anxious to get as far away from Kade Decker as possible. As far away as physical movement would allow, but in her heart she knew she'd see him again…in her nightmare, chasing through the flames after her.

"I PRESSED HER about the fires."

"And?"

"And, nothing." Kade edged out into the corridor, hoping to catch another look at her. His nightie-clad fire angel was even hotter in the flesh, but she was long gone, a fact that intensified the hollow sensation in his chest.

He stepped back into the room, irritated with himself for going primal in the first place.

"Don't worry. I didn't cross your departmental line, but I'd bet she lawyers up."

"Thanks. You've turned her into a hostile. Makes my job harder."

"Take it easy. I like her for this, and if she's our firebug, she's just getting warmed up. It's a compulsion that won't be put out until she's caught. Let's get a search warrant. There's enough probable cause, with the videos and her lack of a reasonable explanation for showing up on scene. I'd also like a copy of her juvenile file. I've got a hunch we'll find something. This compulsion starts early."

"You're sniffing in the wrong direction. Her juvie file is clean. Checked it myself." Nick shrugged his shoulders.

Kade studied his friend, and his hard-line attitude softened a bit. "It would be a shame to lock up a woman like that. She's intelligent, easy on the eyes, has a sense of humor." He paused. All attributes he admired in a woman, but a combination he'd yet to find in his thirty-four years of life.

"On that happy summation—" Nick shrugged his shoulder " —I've gotta go. There's a pile of reports on my desk that have to be processed, today, or the chief is going to blow a gasket. How about we get together tonight for a drink? We can ruminate over the reasons why neither one of us is holding the girl of our dreams."

"I'd like that, but I know why I'm not holding mine." He sobered. "Besides, I'm still helping my mom get settled in her new apartment."

"Rain check then?"

"Yeah." He stared after Nick and sank into the chair trying to make sense of the last half hour.

He'd felt a physical jolt when he'd touched Savannah Dawson's hand, like making contact with a bare wire and having electricity burn through his body to the ground.

It hadn't been an unpleasant sensation, but he wasn't sure what it was.

And then there were her eyes—the eyes he'd somehow imagined were ice-blue were brown. The whole meeting was strange, but stranger still was the feeling of familiarity, as if he somehow knew her.

"Bunk." He stood up, shaking off all the mumbo jumbo in his brain. He'd never seen her in his life. Besides, people were nothing but a compilation of facts. Nothing mystical, unworldly or unobtainable. He'd have the goods on Ms. Dawson. All of them. And when he did, she'd go down easy.

He stepped into the hallway, moving back to the watch room where he'd left his briefcase and cane. But before he reached the door, pain knifed into him, stealing his breath.

Sucking up against the wall for support, he waited for the pain to subside.

Taking a couple of deep breaths, he pushed away, gritted his teeth and put one foot in front of the other. He made it into the tiny cubicle, cursing the Chicago arsonist who'd destroyed his body and his life.

Chapter Two

Kade's fire pager went off in the dark. A series of repetitive beeps signaled an alert and forced him awake in an instant.

He bolted out of bed, looking for his boots, bunker pants and turnout coat, but they weren't there.

Orienting himself in the room, he brushed his face with his hands as reality set in. You could take the fireman out of the station, but instinct would always be a part of him, embedded in his DNA.

A range of emergency tones sounded, right behind the beeps.

Kade stilled, waiting for the information to come over the airwaves.

"Engine Company 44, Ladder company 10, Medical unit 6, Incident Commander Fisk. Please respond to an apartment fire, 816 Forrest Grove Road."

Kade dressed, grabbed his cell phone and dialed 911.

"Montgomery 911, what's your emergency?"

"Fire Investigator Decker, I'll be responding to the apartment fire. Can you repeat the location?"

"Copy that. Eight-One-Six Forrest Grove Road."

Forrest Grove...

Terror sliced into his comprehension.

He closed the phone, adrenaline pumping in his veins, sending his heart rate through the roof.

His mother's apartment building was on fire.

SAVANNAH SAT UP in a cold sweat, a vise of panic around her heart. There was menace in the air, heavy and pervasive.

She threw back the covers and climbed out of bed. In a daze, she pulled on her robe and pushed her feet into her slippers.

She would go to him, she had to go.

KADE TOOK THE CORNER at Forrest Grove and Freemont on two wheels.

The glow of flames against the night sky shook him like an earthquake, opening a deep crevice on his normally smooth facade.

His mom was spending her first night in the building.

A helpless sensation pooled in his chest.

Rolling up to the scene, he assessed the response to keep his sanity.

The top floor of the two-story building was ablaze. Flames licked out of blown windows, acrid smoke turned the night sky blacker. Shaken, soot-covered residents milled on the lawn, but his mother wasn't among them.

Panic constricted his gut as he jumped out of the car and charged toward the incident commander standing near the ladder truck.

"Fisk?"

"Yeah."

"What's the status?" The ladder truck was fully extended, and Kade lifted his gaze to the corner apartment.

His heart stopped.

His mom stood on the balcony of her apartment, waving her arms.

He jetted toward the ladder, biting back a curse, but Fisk blocked his path and shouted an order above the noise of the pump. Strands of fire hose snaked along the ground, hissing and bulging with water. A couple of firemen opened the hose valve and turned the stream on the flames.

"That's my mother up there!"

Fisk turned his gaze to the balcony.

"I'm going up!"

"No way!" The IC didn't budge.

Rage blasted through his veins as he stared into Fisk's sweat-streaked face.

"Turnouts. Where are they?"

Fisk grabbed his shoulder. "I can't let you go." Was it pity he saw in the veteran's eyes, or concern? He didn't know, but it did little to squelch his anger.

A fireman in full turnout gear bound up the ladder, moving toward Kade's mother in quick increments.

Kade let out the breath he'd been holding and stepped back, focused on the man doing the job he'd done so many times he could do it blindfolded.

The fireman covered the distance and reached the balcony in a light spray of water from below that cooled the air around them to a breathable temperature.

His emotions settled the instant he saw his mom climb onto the ladder.

In a matter of minutes, she was being helped down and into his arms. "Thank God you're all right. What happened?"

"I went out on the balcony and the door locked behind me. I couldn't get back in, then the fire started. I don't know how the door got locked."

Uneasiness edged up his spine. "I'll check it out, Mom." He glanced up as the EMTs approached to assess his mother's condition, but when he looked past them, his rage exploded.

There she stood, nightgown and all.

Savannah Dawson.

"Take good care of her." He handed his mother off and charged toward Savannah like a man on fire, his flaming emotions barely contained inside his body.

Was she responsible for this? He'd get it out of her, no matter what.

THE WORD STARTED in a low monotone, grinding against Savannah's eardrums. Over and over the sound repeated, until it turned into a single word.

Clarity flooded her brain and washed her into full consciousness in one jarring instant.

"Savannah! Savannah!"

She pulled free from his grasp, whirled and charged forward, only to come face-to-face with a wall of heat.

Stumbling backward, she slammed into his chest and turned to face the embodiment of her nightmare. Kade Decker. But she wasn't dreaming. She pulled in a breath and nearly choked on the smoky air.

"Where am I?" Her skin tingled as he held her shoulders. She focused on his face in the glow of the flames, the fire in his eyes as emblazoned as the building behind them.

His anger was palpable. She could taste the bitter words on the end of his tongue, feel the excruciating pain that radiated from deep in his body, enraging his nerves to the point of disintegration.

She backed away, severing the physical bond between them, but it left her weak.

"How'd you do it, Dr. Dawson? Do you have an accomplice? Someone to torch the place while you stand outside in your nightie and watch?"

He stepped toward her.

She backed up, lifting her chin, daring him to continue with his tirade. He was judge, jury and extinguisher.

"You've lost it, Decker. I'd never hurt your mom or anyone else."

Her words acted like a slap against his stubbled cheek and he sobered, taking another step toward her.

"You admit you know this is her building? Where'd you get the information?"

She swallowed hard, aware that she'd said too much, drawn his suspicions around her like a strait-jacket. Escape was impossible; he'd never believe she'd gotten the facts from his own mind, from his own thoughts. But the connection worked both ways for some unknown reason, didn't it?

She stared up at him, focusing a statement over and over. *I'm innocent, I didn't do it.*

"So who did?"

His verbal answer to her silent question sent a shiver up her spine.

She turned and bolted through the crowd, racing into the street, hoping for a moment to think. A moment out of his turbulent thoughts, but she could feel him behind her.

She slowed her pace, listening to the decisive slap of his shoes against the asphalt, accentuated by the thud of his cane.

It wasn't any good. She could never mentally outrun him. She stopped and turned to face her tormentor.

KADE SLOWED UP, staring at Savannah Dawson where she stood under a streetlight, haloed in illumination.

She was no angel, even if she looked like one now, but he was about to clip her wings. She had too much information, too many answers for someone with no knowledge about the fires.

He stopped in front of her and squared his shoulders. A hint of mercy stirred in his veins.

She raised her gaze to his, her eyes glimmering in the shallow light.

His breath caught as he stared into her face, seeing her clearly for the first time tonight.

Her eyes were blue. Ice-blue. The color of heaven. But why did she hide them behind colored contact lenses?

Suspicion quickly replaced his surprise. "You know you have to come down to the station?"

"Yeah. I know. I only hope it proves I didn't start this fire, or any of the others."

"How'd you get here, Savannah?"

"I must have walked, but I don't remember doing it. I don't remember anything until I looked up at you a moment ago."

He wasn't sure he believed her, but she'd certainly been out of it when he'd spotted her. He must have yelled her name half a dozen times before she acknowledged him.

"I've heard of sleepwalking crimes. They're rare, but stranger things have happened."

"You think I started this fire while I was sleeping?"

He couldn't answer her outright. It was a bizarre

idea and he didn't believe it to be a fact. Suspicion fisted in his gut. "Let's go. Forensics needs to process you."

"Wait a minute. I'm not an object—"

"But you are a suspect." Fear flared in her eyes and he felt her helpless reaction for an instant, then the odd sensation vanished. "They'll take your night-gown and robe, check for residue. Chances are you'll be home before dawn."

"Great. Let's get it over with, prove I'm inno-cent." She swallowed, and he felt her apprehension. His heart softened. "It'll work out. It's a simple pro-cedure, painless."

"I know."

"There'll be a squad car to take you downtown." He grasped her elbow as they started back toward the scene. A tingling sensation worked its way up his arm, but he didn't let go of her. He couldn't risk losing her this time.

"I need to check on my mother."

"She's going to be fine. She was rescued in plenty of time."

He wanted to press her further. Her information was too strong to be coincidental. It sounded more like firsthand knowledge.

They reached the ambulance and he looked into the back where his mother sat on the gurney, holding an oxygen mask over her mouth and nose.

She lowered it when she saw him. "How many times do I have to tell them, I'm fine!"

"Relax, Mom, they're just doing their job."

"They want to take me to the hospital."

"Let them. I'll be down in a couple of hours to pick you up. Bring you back out to the house."

She shook her head in disgust. "Not much choice, I guess."

"Tell me exactly what happened."

"I went out onto the balcony looking for mine an, but when I tried the sliding glass door to go back in, it wouldn't budge. I must have spent an hour out there trying to decide what to do. That's when I saw the glow of the fire through the drapes. I wish I could tell you more."

"It's okay." He patted her hand. "I'll see you in a bit."

She put the mask back on and waved him off.

He turned to find Savannah standing a short distance away, her hands in her robe pockets, staring at the smoldering building.

He was drawn to her and moved in closer, sensing a degree of fear escalating in her body.

"What is it?" He put his hand on her back, making her jump.

"He's here. Watching."

"Who's watching?" He turned her, clasping her shoulders in his hands.

"The man who did this." She suddenly went limp and rocked forward.

He caught her or she would have collapsed, but the sudden contact jolted him, infusing his body with a sensation of weightlessness.

She regained her footing and the feeling inside him dissipated.

"How do you know that?" He stared at the crowd of bystanders, searched the faces, scrutinized anyone who didn't fit, but they all fit. Many of them he'd known from his childhood growing up in Montgomery.

"Do you see him? Can you tell me who he is?" He whispered the questions in her ear, catching a whiff of vanilla on her skin.

"He's not in the crowd, and I don't know who he is."

"Then how do you know he's here?"

She looked up at him, and his breath caught in his throat. She was beautiful, and for an instant the outside world fell away. Desire raced through his system, sucking him into a tornado of sensation that spun him around and spit him out.

"I can't see him…I feel him."

Kade raked his hand over his head and tried to translate her words into something that made sense. "I wish to hell I knew what you were talking about."

She grabbed his arm and pulled him around to the side of the ambulance. "I'm psychic. There, I've said it. If you can make sense of it, great. If you can't, too bad."

He was ready with a humorous comeback, but her

teeth were clenched, her face serious, her expression close to desperation. Something he knew far too much about these days.

"I had no idea." What was he supposed to do? Indulge her fantasy? "So where is he? Give me a direction, something to go on. That's what you do, right?"

She closed her eyes and extended her hands, palms facing forward. Like something out of a science-fiction movie, she turned in a circle.

Kade held his breath, hope knotting his nerves together, but reality set in as she finished her pirouette and opened her eyes.

This was nuts. He squeezed his cane handle, considering her odd demeanor with skepticism.

"Over your right shoulder, there's a grove of trees. He's hiding there."

Should he believe her? Or should he stuff her in a squad car and get to work on this investigation using material he could see with his own eyes?

"Fine, you can discount my empathic observation, or you can check it out for yourself."

How had she known about his doubts, or how deep they ran inside his head? "I'll humor you this once, Savannah. Then you're going downtown."

If his statement frightened her, it didn't show on her face. Her slight, "you'll see" smile, however, bothered him. She could have staged the scene to throw the investigation in another direction, away from her, but there was only one way to find out.

He turned, spotted the grove of trees and limped toward them.

The stagnant air was heavy with humidity and smoke. He made his way across the span of lawn to the point where the grove stood as a gateway into a densely wooded area, thick with water oak and pine.

The light stopped where the tangle of vegetation began. He hesitated. The hair on his neck bristled and oddly enough, he could feel her watching him, nudging him forward, begging him to accept her proof. Believe her claim…take the bait.

He shook it off and stepped into the grove, listening for the sound of movement, anything that would indicate he wasn't alone.

Irritation jetted through him as he moved deeper into the stand, determined to disprove her information.

The grass rustled to his left.

He focused on a cluster of shadows and stepped toward the sound, ready to scare the hell out of whatever small creature had the unfortunate luck of crossing his path.

A flurry of movement disoriented him. He heard footsteps behind him, but it was too late.

Someone slammed an object against the back of his head and his world went black.

SAVANNAH'S MIND went blank for an instant.

Kade was in trouble.

In a full sprint, she ran to the grove, pausing near

the overgrown opening, before pushing into the center of the trees.

The light was minimal, but she could just make out the shape of a body on the ground. "Kade!"

He moaned. "Get out! Run!"

"He's gone." She knelt next to him, helping him into a sitting position. She brushed his shoulder with her hand, feeling a degree of his pain.

"Looks like you and your mom get to share an ambulance ride tonight."

"I don't need an ambulance. I need the guy who just tried to take my head off."

"I should have warned you."

"You knew this was going to happen?"

"Not exactly, but I felt his desperation when you cornered him."

"I'd like to say I believe you, but…"

"Save it, Decker. I eat skeptics for breakfast and I've dined on the finest. Why do you think I hide my abilities and my eye color? It's to protect myself from people like you." She picked up his cane and stood up, feeling exhausted.

"Can you get up on your own?" She already knew he could, but she helped him to his feet anyway, placing the cane in his hand.

"What's wrong with your hip?"

"I was in an accident."

"Is it painful?" She knew the answer; she'd tapped into the sensation.

"For the most part, yeah. But I'm working through it."

She pulled his arm around her shoulder and they stumbled out of the grove in silence.

Nick Brandt spotted them and crossed the lawn, a frown on his face. "This isn't summer camp kids. It's no time to be sneaking off into the woods."

Kade grinned at his friend, but didn't take his arm off Savannah's shoulder. He liked the way she fit next to him, liked the tension he felt trapped inside her body screaming to get out. It was sweet torture with a twist. The contact made him feel better, eased his pain.

"You'll like what we found on our foray. A voyeur with a club. He was watching."

"I'll get a team in here. If he left anything behind, we'll find it."

"Then there's Dr. Dawson." He purposely stared down at her. "She arrived on scene in her nightie again. Better check her for residue."

"He really needs the bump on his head examined. It's affecting his brain."

He liked the glimmer of challenge he saw in her cool blue eyes.

"I'm sorry, doc, but you'll have to come with me."

"Gladly." She pulled free of him. "If it proves I'm not your firebug."

Kade watched her walk away and be helped into the backseat of a black-and-white, satisfied when it pulled away.

"Better get that knot looked at, buddy." Nick Brandt moved up next to him.

"I'll live. Why didn't you clue me in about Dr. Dawson's…interesting talent?"

Nick shrugged, shoving his hands into his pockets. "Would you have believed me?"

"Probably not."

"Do you remember that kidnapping case a couple of years ago, the little girl who went missing down in Mobile? Her kidnapper was in a car accident shortly after the ransom drop and died before he could tell us where the girl was?"

"Yeah, made the news in Chicago." Kade fingered the back of his head, feeling for blood.

"Dr. Savannah Dawson found her."

"No kidding…"

"From the station downtown. She's the real deal, buddy. An honest-to-goodness, credible psychic."

Kade sucked in a long breath and let it out, trying to get his head around the details. "Is that your only case?"

"There are dozens just like it. She's my department's secret weapon. I can't disclose every case she's worked. If the media got hold of it, we'd take a beating. We're already being scrutinized on a daily basis. It'd be fuel on fire."

"You're right. And she said as much tonight. I got the impression she's been ridiculed for her talent."

"Yeah. This city's got a knack for putting folks through the grinder for being different."

Admiration stirred in his mind. Savannah Dawson was a survivor. He liked that.

"Can I ask you something?"

"Shoot."

"You said she grew up in Atlanta and moved here five years ago."

"Yeah."

"Where was she born?"

"She's a native. Born right here in Montgomery."

A chill screamed through his body, waking up a long buried memory.

"I've got to get down to the hospital, check on my mom. I'll be back to have a look as soon as this mother cools off."

"No problem. Maybe we'll have some forensics on your assailant by the time you get back."

Kade squeezed his cane and limped toward his car. Gritting his teeth, he climbed in and fired the engine.

He'd known Savannah Dawson once upon a time, as sure as he knew his own name. Now he had to confirm it.

Chapter Three

Kade tried to force up the sliding glass door latch, but it was melted in place. It proved one thing. His mom had been locked out when the fire started.

Relief coursed through his veins as he turned back into the charred apartment where the arsonist had left his mark in the middle of the room. A point of origin that had dropped from the ceiling onto a tile. Too bad the intense heat had destroyed the incendiary device itself, leaving him little to go on.

Fear worked its way into his mind. His mother's home had been targeted, but had she? Most firebugs didn't give away get-out-of-fire-free cards or lock their victims out of a fire.

Don Watson from the crime lab entered the apartment with his kit. "Want that door?"

"Yeah. The lock mechanism is of particular interest. My mom claims when she tried it from the outside, it was locked. The fire started not long after that. I want to know if it failed, or if someone intentionally pushed the lever down."

"You got it."

Kade made his way through the apartment, flicking his flashlight beam over every inch. Most of the items he remembered from his childhood were here, covered with soot and water, a total loss.

Was Alice Decker the target or a random victim? Frustration threaded through him, stitching up a solution he could live with. He wouldn't take risks with her safety; he wanted her to leave town, go to visit relatives, get as far away from Montgomery as she could until he figured this out and put the arsonist behind bars.

He paused at his mom's bedroom door and shined the light inside. The beam swept across her bed, and surprise squeezed in his chest. He pulled the beam back to the bed where a long lump lay with the covers pulled over it. His mom's full-length body pillow. A therapeutic apparatus she used to support her limbs when she lay on her side.

Had the arsonist mistaken the lump for Alice Decker?

Fear twisted around his nerves, giving voice to his self-doubt. He couldn't afford to screw this up.

"Hey, Decker. The door's open."

Kade turned off his flashlight and returned to the living room. "What's it look like inside?"

"Broken. When your mom closed it, the latch

dropped, locking her out. It's missing the spring that holds the latch up."

"That failure saved her life. Whoever started this fire thought she was in bed. He or she had no way of knowing Mom was on the balcony when the fire took off. Let's dust. Maybe a print survived the inferno, and I want to access the attic."

"Will do."

Kade leaned on his cane and took a deep breath, but he couldn't relax, couldn't pull it together when there was a maniac out there setting fires. But how was his mom involved? Was she a random target? In the right place at the wrong time?

He studied the burn pattern in the middle of the living room floor. "Did you find anything left here?"

"Nothing readily visible, but there was a clump of fibrous material." Watson shuffled around in his collection kit and pulled out a clear plastic bag. "It could be part of the melted carpet, or the ceiling tile, but it stayed intact. I'm going to analyze it under the microscope, get a look at the weave pattern to determine what it is."

Kade took the bag and held it up to the light coming in through the open sliding glass door. The clump of fiber was knitted together in a circular pattern.

"Looks like a filter." He held the bag out for Watson to inspect.

Don turned on his flashlight and examined the evidence. "You're right. It could be what's left of a cigarette filter. That could be evidence of an incendiary device. I'll run it through the tests, get something definitive."

"Thanks." Kade took one last look around the burned-out room and hobbled to the door. His hip was killing him. He needed to slam back a couple of pain meds to survive the afternoon.

The search warrant for Savannah Dawson's house would be coming down within the hour, and he wanted to be there when it was executed.

SAVANNAH GLANCED UP from her notepad and considered the patient sitting across the desk from her, but her attention sagged as he blew his nose on a tissue.

"I'm sorry this upsets you, George, but you need to come to terms with the breakup. Once you let the painful memories go, you can begin to heal."

"I know, but it's the hardest thing I've ever had to do. She meant so much to me."

She pushed the box of Kleenex toward him. He pulled out two more and dabbed at his nose.

Changing the subject might get them past George's tearful stage, something that happened at the beginning of each session, but today it had gone on too long. She'd have to properly analyze it, maybe contact a colleague and get his take.

George had an extreme obsessive personality and trouble controlling his compulsions. It was one of the worst cases she'd ever encountered, but he was making progress, she thought.

"Are you feeling better?"

"Yes."

"Good. That's our time for today. Have Charlene make you an appointment for next week at our regular time, and I'm sorry I missed our 10:00 a.m. yesterday."

He reluctantly got up from the chair. "I should come to see you more often."

Savannah stood up. "More problems?"

He dropped his gaze, then looked up again. "I like you. You make me feel comfortable and understood. You've helped me get through this tough time in my life."

"Two hours a week is sufficient. You're making wonderful progress."

George Welte nodded his head, moseyed to the door and gave her one last glance over the top of his thick glasses before he slid out of the room, closing the door behind him.

Savannah sat back down in her chair, her mind absent. She was no good to her patients or herself in this state. Since surrendering her nightgown, robe and slippers at the police station last night, she hadn't been able to get Kade Decker off her mind. He was like a CD looped out on the same song, and she couldn't stop playing him. Then there was the search warrant, probably being executed at this very moment. A physical manifestation of his mental determination to prove her guilt.

She chewed her bottom lip and considered what they'd find. Lighter fluid was a given. In the garage, outside on the patio next to the barbecue. Nothing could be read into it; half the residents of the city could be suspects if he chose to focus on lighter fluid.

Fear raked her nerves. She'd felt his determination, been infused with his surety of her guilt, but there was a boundary there, too. A level of integrity that encompassed everything he said and did. She'd just have to let the lack of evidence confirm it for him.

She stood up and gazed out the third-story window at the rear parking lot below.

The heat outside was suffocating, the index off the charts. A watery sheen of vapor flamed up from the asphalt.

She watched George Welte walk to his red Mercedes coupe, climb inside and drive away.

If only she could shut Kade out, turn off the receptors inside her head, maybe she could get some peace. Her only other option was to deal with it. Figure it out. Find the catalyst for their connection. It had to be buried somewhere in the past. Maybe it was time for a resurrection.

She pushed the button on her intercom. "Charlene? Could you come in here for a moment?"

The door pushed open and her secretary entered. "What's my afternoon look like?"

"You've got a three o'clock and a five."

"Call them and reschedule for next Monday."

"Sure." Charlene disappeared back into the outer office, leaving her with a tangle of thoughts to sort out.

She'd never shared a psychic bond like the one she was currently sharing with Kade Decker. But how had it happened? She'd never met him before yesterday, and suddenly they were locked in some sort of cosmic union. Fused in thought and feeling, while he sucked the energy from her body every time they touched.

"Damn." She was beginning to scare herself, and just when she thought she had this psychic thing wired, laced up in a neat little package that she could control and understand.

She plopped into her chair, rocked back, closed her eyes and concentrated, practicing a form of self-hypnosis she'd shared with many of her patients.

Like a silent movie playing in her head, she perused the last forty-eight hours. Gradually, her thoughts pushed farther and farther back until an image slammed into her brain.

She bolted forward, excitement churning her insides, spinning off snippets of detail long forgotten.

Her hand shook as she grabbed her purse out of the desk drawer, left the office and headed for a rendezvous with an ancient memory.

SAVANNAH DROVE into the old section of town, past rows of mature oaks and old row houses.

She hadn't been back since she'd been removed

by protective services on April 18th. Twenty-eight years ago.

Summoning her courage, she turned onto Palm Street and slowed her speed, taking in the sensation of familiarity that teased her nerves and edged her into the past.

A past that had been wonderful up to a point, the point where everything had changed and her destiny had spun out of control.

The house still belonged to her. Her mother had left it to her after she died, but it had been used as a rental ever since.

According to the agency, there was a new tenant moving in, but she hoped he wasn't there yet.

She pulled into the driveway and killed the engine.

A lump squeezed in her stomach. She felt tears sting the backs of her eyes, remembering the frightened little girl she'd once been.

Breathing through the moment, she climbed out of the car, letting the memories consume her as she stepped onto the cracked cement.

Some were happy. Peddling her bike, listening to the click-clack of the cracks under her tires. Doing cartwheels and somersaults until she collapsed in exhaustion.

Then it had all ended, and hell began.

She pushed the painful images aside and headed for the backyard.

Her mood lightened as she walked around to the

side of the house, intent on the memory she'd rousted half an hour ago.

The gate squeaked open, and she stepped through into the neglected yard.

The ghosts from her past were all here, resting comfortably.

She let the spring-loaded gate slap shut, moving along the fence, raking her fingertips over the rough board slats before stopping three-quarters of the way down the fence line.

This was the spot, she decided as she knelt down in the warm grass. The very spot where she and Kade's lives had become intertwined. The how, she knew, but the why was much more illusive.

The four-inch knothole near the bottom of the board was weathered but just as she remembered it, only lower to the ground.

She'd been five years old that year. The year the boy next door had become her only friend. The only child on the block who didn't think she was a freak, with a crazy lady for a mother. The memory was poignant and drove sadness into her heart.

She crouched down on all fours, ringed the knot with her finger and put her eye to the hole like she'd done as a child.

The yard next door looked the same. Short chopped grass, well kept. Abundant flowerbeds teaming with gladiolas, iris and snapdragons. Stuck in a time warp, like her wardrobe, she decided as she stared at the same set of urns flanking the back patio and overflowing with bright fuchsia petunias.

A wind chime tinkled, challenged by the hint of breeze stirring the muggy July air.

Sweat crept from her hairline at the nape of her neck and tickled down her back, but she was mesmerized. Glued to the past.

A shadow descended on the other side of the fence, and the tiny portal was blocked.

She swallowed, staring back at the hazel eye gazing at her through the knothole. The iris was ringed by tiny golden flecks, the color as smooth as dark honey.

"Savannah?" Kade's voice cut into her hearing and she froze. Swaddled in the fabric of time. Transported back to the single thing that had joined them for twenty-eight years.

A kids' game. An equal exchange of DNA. The origin of their psychic connection.

Blood brothers.

"Kade." She swallowed and pulled back, relief liquefying in her veins. She wasn't crazy; she was perfectly sane.

"Stay put, I'm coming over."

She stood up, waiting for him, glad when the gate opened and he limped toward her, cane in hand.

"When did you figure it out?" he asked, stopping next to her.

"An hour ago."

"I knew last night, the minute I saw your eyes. I've never forgotten them. I verified your name with my mom. She's got a memory like an elephant. Reminded me of the whole story."

He touched her arm, sending a jolt of electricity through her. She looked up into his face, as if seeing him for the first time.

The boy she remembered had turned into a man. His dominant features were still there. A distinct jawline, expressive eyes, but time and some sort of tragedy had changed his insides.

"Which story would that be? There are so many." A hint of discomfort jabbed her heart as she swallowed her anticipation. Her memories of that day were cloudy; maybe his could help to drive the fog away.

"Children's services came and took you. Mom remembered the insignia on the car…then someone from the state came for your mother."

Sorrow, deep and raw, penetrated her soul. She'd been given the information by her adoptive parents. It had been so long ago that the story had lost its edge, but hearing Kade describe it brought it all back.

"They said she was crazy, that she couldn't handle raising a child. But they were wrong. She was psychic, not mental. Did she fight? Did she struggle to stay?"

"I don't know."

Savannah hung her head, haunted by the whispers of the past. The despair she'd felt, the confusion and loneliness.

"What happened to her after they took her?"

His concern wrapped around her; she could feel it like a caress. "She died several years later in a mental institution. I was adopted by the Dawsons, and here I am." She'd left out a dark decade, but it didn't matter. There was nothing there she cared to revisit.

"You still own this place?"

"Yeah. My mom left it to me. It's a rental right now. What about your house?"

"My mom's place is going on the market…well, it was until the fire. She's back until she finds another apartment building."

"I'm sorry."

"I'm not. It's home."

"Do you remember doing it?"

He hung his head, then looked up. "I remember the jolt, and I think I supplied the razor blade and you brought the Band-Aids."

She had to smile now as she pulled the full memory into focus. The trouble she'd had slicing into her own finger without flinching, being shocked when blood oozed out of the cut. Feeling a wondrous sense of belonging as they locked their fingers together, mixing their blood and making a promise to one another. "A couple of silly kids trying to stay linked forever."

"It worked, didn't it?"

She swallowed, overcome with emotion, lost in the odd sensation generating between them. "Yeah, better than we could have imagined, but I'm not sure I like free passage on your train of thought."

"And you think it's a thrill ride for me? I'm new at this. What do you say we get a cold drink and you give me some pointers on mind reading?"

"I'd like that." She let him take her elbow and steer her toward the gate. It took everything she had, but she put up a mental wall between them. She didn't want to know his thoughts and feelings about that day before he verbalized them. She wanted it fresh, she wanted to hear them firsthand.

When they reached the gate, he pulled her up short and stared down into her face. "All I want to know is why you hide the color of your eyes."

"It keeps people from freaking out. I got tired of the stares. It was easier to disguise them with brown contacts than to take the gasps of horror, like I was some sort of demon child from the *Village of the Damned,* able to melt small children with a single glare."

"I understand. If I remember right, they matched my best cleary marble. I always thought they were cool, but it wasn't something I could explain to my buddies. They would have kicked me out of the fort."

"Thanks for that."

"You're welcome."

"Let me get my purse and lock my car."

Kade held the gate open and followed her into the driveway, enjoying the sway of her hips, but the sightseeing ended when he spotted a pickup truck parked across the street and watched a lanky man climb out and move in their direction.

"Oh, no!"

"What is it?" He refocused on Savannah.

"It's gone! My purse is gone." Disappointment choked her voice.

"You're sure you didn't take it into the yard?"

"Yes."

He took her arm. "Let's call the police. File a report. The sooner you cancel your credit cards, the better."

"Hi. Are you the landlord?"

Kade glanced up at the man who'd walked across the street and now stood in the driveway next to them.

"No. I think you want Ms. Dawson."

"If she owns this yellow house, then I guess I do."

He didn't like the way the man devoured Savannah with his gaze or the satisfied smile that followed.

"Ms. Dawson, I'm Todd Coleman, your new tenant."

Savannah looked up at the jean-clad man addressing her and offering his hand. She shook it, momentarily forgetting her missing purse and key ring.

"Doctor Savannah Dawson. Pleased to meet you, but I don't have a key. You'll have to stop by the rental agency for that."

"Done." He pulled a key out of his pocket. "Picked it up this morning. This is a great place. I knew I had to have it the first time I saw it."

"You're planning to move in today?"

"Yeah."

Kade felt caution sluice in his veins, but he couldn't locate a source for the feeling. Savannah's new tenant was slick, and he wasn't sure that there wasn't some jealousy mixed in with his concern.

"Great...Mr. Coleman, is it?" Kade eyed him tentatively.

"Yeah."

"Any chance you saw someone around Ms. Dawson's car in the last ten minutes?"

Kade gauged his reaction, but he had a poker face under a layer of tanned skin.

"As a matter of fact, I did see a guy hanging around. I think he was driving a red car...high-end. Why? What's the problem?"

"Ms. Dawson's purse has been stolen."

"Damn. That's tough."

The reaction sounded genuine and Kade relaxed, letting go of his caution.

"I see you work for the fire department. Are you a fireman?" Coleman pointed at the insignia on the department vehicle parked in the driveway next door.

"I used to be." Disappointment gelled in his veins. "I'm an arson investigator now."

"That's cool. You don't get to race into burning buildings anymore, but you get to figure out who torched them?"

"Something like that."

"I always wanted to get on with the department."

"Really." Kade studied Coleman's frame. "You should look into it. The department can always use new recruits. Now, if you'll excuse us, we need to call the police and file a report."

"If you need me to tell the cops what I saw, you know where to find me."

"I have a spare key at home. I'll get my car out of the driveway later today," Savannah said.

"No problem." Todd Coleman turned toward the street.

Kade took Savannah's elbow and walked her toward his house. He could feel Coleman's eyes on his back, but he resisted the urge to turn around. Instead, he zoned on the feel of his fingers against her bare skin, absorbing the odd transfer of current from her body into his.

That's when it hit him. He was walking normally. The pain in his hip had subsided.

She wasn't only psychic—she was a living, breathing, pain annihilator.

HE BRUSHED HIS HAND across the pillow and closed his eyes, imagining her head on it, her hair fanned out in contrast against the crisp white linen.

Pulling in a deep breath, he honed in on her scent in the room, her room, a place he'd been many times…but never with her. Breaking in felt so wrong, but he knew where the spare key was.

He sobered, opened his eyes and tamped down the irritation flaring in his veins.

She would come to care for him. He already knew her secret. Coaxed it, fed it. Her affection couldn't be far behind.

His heart drummed in his chest as he wandered into the bathroom, bent on somehow telling her, making her understand the flames were for her.

Then it would only be a matter of time before she recognized how much he wanted her. She would return his love. Lie in his arms until dawn penetrated the night....

Chapter Four

Savannah stared at the front of her house from the passenger seat of Kade's vehicle.

It was late, dark, and she hadn't bothered to turn on the porch light. A shiver rattled through her. Leaving her purse and keys unprotected in the car had been a stupid mistake. Who knew a lapse in judgment would leave her feeling so vulnerable.

"Let's go inside. I'll check it out, and we'll wait for the locksmith to show up."

She was glad Kade was with her. "Works for me, but I'm sure everything is fine. If he did use my key to get inside, he'd probably steal items he could pawn and be out of there before he got caught."

"Probably."

She didn't like the note of uncertainty in his voice. She climbed out of the car and made her way up the front walkway with Kade next to her.

"I keep a spare key in the flower pot." She bent over, fished the key out of the large terra-cotta pot, brimming with flowers, and dusted the potting soil off with her fingertips.

"Now that's some kind of security."

"This is a quiet neighborhood. This key is perfectly safe in that pot, and I refuse to believe differently."

"Huh. A Pollyanna. Too bad the thieves only want to jerk on your pigtails, while they make off with your stuff."

She slid the key into the knob, apprehension bunching her muscles as she glared at him in the dark. It wasn't wrong to think the best of people, unless her vibes told her otherwise, but she'd have to be more careful in the future.

Her tension released with the decisive click of the lock. Turning the knob, she stepped into the foyer and pulled in a deep breath, but her relief was short-lived.

The air held an unfamiliar scent, a tangle of male cologne and sweat.

Pausing, she fiddled for the light switch and flipped it on. "Do you smell that?"

"Smell what?"

"Aftershave." She pulled in another breath, but the scent had dissipated.

Kade closed the door and shot her a concerned glance. "I don't smell anything, but then this isn't my house. I wouldn't know one foreign odor from another."

She moved toward him, determined to find out if he was the source. "Did you shower this morning?"

"Like clockwork, darlin'."

Warmth crept into her cheeks. "Mind if I check?"

"Be my guest." He raised his hands in a surrender position, a slow mysterious smile on his lips.

She circled him. Sucking in the air around him. His scent was earthy and seductive. Miles away from the smell she'd encountered moments ago. His essence invaded her senses, taking her prisoner as a rush of desire revved her body. It was anything but offensive; in fact, she could easily imagine holding his shirt to her nose and breathing him in, like she'd seen her mother do before she'd put one of her dad's shirts into the washing machine.

She swallowed, caught off guard by the intimate images inside her head and hoping he hadn't intercepted them.

"No. Definitely not you. But someone has been in my house. Maybe we should call the police, again."

"Let's have a look around."

She gazed into Kade's face and tried to relax. He was as tense as she was, but why?

He could easily take on anything or anyone. She knew that about him. Felt it in her soul. *He was strong and lean, muscle, bone and determination, but something held him back. Kept him from his strengths. Her gaze drifted to his cane.*

His knuckles blanched white on the top of the crook and his reasons hit her like a physical punch.

"You can stop now."

"Stop what?" She walked into the living room, flipping on lights as she went, knowing full well what he meant.

"Digging for information in my head. I've figured out how to keep you out."

"Really?" She slipped into the kitchen and turned on the dual fluorescent over the island.

A chill pushed through her body, stalling her in place.

She could feel Kade inches from her back, feel the whisper of his breath against her hair.

"What is it?"

"That." She pointed to the double place settings neatly arranged on the island. She leaned into him, pulling some of his strength around her.

"I'd like to think you did this beforehand, sort of a premonition that we'd be here tonight, alone. But I'll take your caution to mean that's a no?"

Fear laced around her heart and she tried to smile at his joke, but couldn't quite grasp the humor. The place settings were harmless; it was the reasoning behind them that worried her.

"Let's call a locksmith. If he used my stolen keys to get in, I can't let it happen again."

Kade moved past her and picked up the phone book off the workstation. "Take it easy, Savannah. He might have left a print. We'll get Nick's team in here. Maybe they can find something."

"Are you kidding? Look at the settings, they're

perfect." She judged the distance between the plates and the edge of the counter. "I'd bet you both plates are exactly one inch from the edge of the island. The silverware is laid out to perfection. Even the napkins are fanned in an outstanding accordion fold."

"So the guy's a waiter in a five-star. He still broke into your house."

"Correction, entered with a key. Do you really think there will be any prints?"

Kade leaned against the counter and considered her dead-on observations. She had a point, a rather sharp one. Whoever had put the settings together was the son of Miss Manners or an anal waiter on his night off. Either way, he had a bad feeling about it.

"Don't know, but I'm calling Brandt, a locksmith and the takeout joint, in that order." He threw her a sideways glance and saw her smile. The gesture set his heart rate on the fast track. He turned back to the phone, punched in Nick's number and gave him the info, listening to Savannah rattle off her address from over his shoulder. He hung up the phone and turned toward her. "Chinese?"

"Guess." She smiled. A seductive grin that dared him to find the answer without words. He could really get into this mind-reading stuff.

"The Jade Dragon. Honey walnut shrimp with fried rice and egg flower soup."

"Exactly. You catch on quick. How did you do that?"

"It's underlined right here on the menu." He

picked up the soy-stained piece of paper and handed it to her, but a wave of disappointment sideswiped him and vanished along with her smile.

"I'm sorry. I didn't know it would mean anything to you."

"It's not a game, Kade."

He mentally tried to hide his doubt in a labyrinth of thought, but he watched her stiffen and walk over to the kitchen sink, pull a glass down from the cupboard and fill it with water.

This thing scared the hell out of him. He had enough trouble just keeping his head in the game of life these days. Now he had to share space with her? *What would keep him from having a cranial explosion?*

"It's okay." She turned toward him. "I understand. It takes some getting used to. You can put up walls. It's as simple as blocking access. A mental no, as it were. And no, your head isn't going to explode. I don't want to clean up gray matter. It doesn't match my tile."

He shoved aside his annoyance and refocused, effectively blocking her out. "So, Chinese and I'm taking the couch?"

"Unless that's tonight's special, no."

He stepped toward her, lifting his mental gate just long enough so she could feel his concern before he closed it again.

"As long as Mister Manners is leaving his calling card at your house, I think you should have someone around. And since we seem to be so in tune with one another—" he moved to within six inches of her face "—I'm the man for the job. I've got a weapon handy." He gestured to his cane, leaning against the counter. "And the know-how to use it. If the creep doesn't come back by week's end, you can put me out with the old newspapers. Deal?"

Try as he might, he couldn't get into her mind. She had more experience with this thing than he did, a fact that irritated him, but he was a quick study. He'd have her thoughts down pat and read in no time, not to mention the physical advantages of touching her.

"Deal."

The tension coiled around his shoulder blades relaxed and he stared down at her, intent on the shape and shade of her lips.

He rode a brief instant of need that rushed through his body like a tidal wave, only to crash ashore somewhere near his heart.

To deny she was beautiful, to look at her as nothing more than a childhood friend, just wasn't in him. Not tonight....

He lowered his mouth to hers, adrift in a holey lifeboat and sinking fast.

Their lips met and he drowned in the urgent rush of need sucking him under.

Her lips were soft, welcoming, and he was hungry.

She opened for him, he explored her with his tongue. Tasting the sweetness of her mouth, wanting more, until the kiss hit a crescendo and they pulled apart.

He tried to find a normal breathing rhythm in the storm's aftermath, but it was elusive. He stepped away from her, a move that offered some relief for his jagged nerves, but his lingering lust was unquenchable and his body hummed from the contact.

"Deal's off." Savannah put several feet between them, but distance couldn't stop the pounding of her heart or the catch of her breath deep in her chest as she stared at him, feeling the level of chaos in his mind and body.

Kade leaned against the counter, his arms crossed over his chest. "I'll stay until Nick is done. You're sure you'll be all right?"

"Yeah. The creep probably won't come back."

"Probably not." He tried to relax, but it was useless. He couldn't help but travel the road of caution winding through his mind. There was something dangerous out there. He didn't know how he knew, he just knew. And as long as he could still suck air and get around, he was going to protect Savannah Dawson, whether she wanted him to or not.

"So…did you bag my starter fluid today after the hunt?"

The question grated on his nerves and he straightened. "I was wondering when you'd ask me about the warrant. As much as I wanted to close this case, I have to admit I was wrong."

"That's big of you." She attempted to scour his

mind, find out why he'd gotten the warrant in the first place, but he'd shut her out.

"I'm a man who likes facts, Savannah. We just didn't find any of them here." He panned the room with his gaze, before returning it to her.

She could feel heat creep into her cheeks, but she returned his stare. "I suppose you went after my juvenile file?"

"Yeah."

She dropped her stare, mustering the courage to continue, but she couldn't. She'd carried the dark secret for so long she couldn't dislodge it from her mind, much less voice it.

He must have picked up on her turmoil, because he turned his back on her and moved to the sink.

"You lucked out. Brandt claimed you didn't have a juvenile record." He turned toward her. "But he didn't look under the correct last name. Did he?"

She pulled in several deep breaths before her throat squeezed shut. He would never accept her reasons for doing it. His job was to catch pyros like her, not tolerate what they did.

"I don't have anything to hide."

Kade pushed away from the counter. "Really. We'll see when the record comes in. I just want to make sure."

Fear and regret wrapped around her nerves.

In a week, maybe days, he'd know the truth about her.

She couldn't hide anymore.

Chapter Five

Kade watched Savannah's bedroom light go out and checked his watch: 3:22 a.m. The cops hadn't found a single unsub print, the locksmith was overpaid and the takeout food they'd ordered was sitting in his stomach like a hunk of lead. Still, he couldn't beat back the worry that throbbed in his veins.

He was sure Savannah's line of work took her swimming in a pool of wackos, any one of them capable of an obsession that could turn deadly. Whoever had set up the romantic dinner scene, was someone she knew. Obsession was rarely a symptom of random contact.

He pulled the lever on the side of the seat and took it back a couple of notches. He planned to stay put outside her house tonight. He was just being male, as she'd so eloquently informed him, but he couldn't shake the sensation of her palpable fear as it had rushed over him, betraying her true feelings.

Kade closed his eyes, intending to rest them for a few moments before he again went on alert, but the sound of his fire pager beeping in the closed space of the car slammed him awake.

"Dammit." He must have dozed off. He'd sworn to stay alert. He glanced at Savannah's house, torn between need and duty. She'd promised to lock the bedroom door and put the portable phone on the pillow next to her. She was safe, wasn't she?

"Engine Company 53. Company 44. Ladder Company 10. Medical Units 6 and 10. IC Fisk. Respond to a fully involved apartment fire. 4591 Ogden Street."

Kade's blood ran cold as he turned the key and fired the engine. The address was less than a mile away.

RED-HOT FLAMES flashed and flickered, burning through her clothes. Heat seared her skin and lungs as she fought to breathe.

She tried to pull away; then he was there, moving toward her through the fire, but a shadow held him back, the blade of an ax suspended above his head, cutting the air as it sliced toward him.

"No!"

Savannah bolted up in bed, panic in her veins. Her breath coming in rapid succession, keeping time with her pulse.

She would go to him. She had to go.

KADE HAMMERED his fist against the roof of the car in frustration as he took in the horrific scene.

Since arriving at the apartment fire half an hour

ago, he'd witnessed the extrication of five victims, but the structure contained ten units and most of the residents had been asleep when the blaze broke out.

There was death in the air. Death and frustration and sorrow.

He pounded the roof again, trying to ease the pent-up anger that circled in his veins along with his blood, a tangle of helpless emotion that threatened to destroy him.

It was arson. He'd known it the moment he'd rolled up on the fire and found ten points of origin, one for every front door. One for every family that slept behind that door, cut off from an escape route by a sick individual who knew they were inside.

His rage solidified and turned to determination as he leaned on his cane and gritted his teeth. He'd nail the SOB responsible for this if it was the last thing he ever did.

Kade moved toward Fisk, purpose and pain in his long strides. Calm took over his nerves, blocking out the horror around him. He was no good to the victims if he couldn't control his rage. If he couldn't focus on the evidence.

"Decker!" Incident Commander Fisk shouted over the roar of the draft pumps pushing water to the flames.

Kade pulled up short and watched the fireman approach. "What's the status?"

"We vented the roof, but she's tricky. The place

has been smoldering for hours. We're lucky it didn't flash. Hurt somebody."

He had to agree. A smoldering fire only needed a breath of air to explode into an out-of-control firestorm.

"Any survivors on the second floor?" He knew by the look in Fisk's eyes there wasn't anyone left alive up there.

"The smoke got 'em."

Kade's rage bubbled close to the surface, but he pulled it back and filled the void with resolve.

"Let me know when it's out. I want in there as soon as possible."

"You got it." Fisk turned back to the fire and Kade limped back to his car for his camera.

The odds were good that the bastard was in the crowd standing in the street. He couldn't let another minute go by without getting some shots.

Already, a uniformed officer was running a strip of crime-scene tape to keep the curious at bay.

He ducked under the tape and positioned himself next to a tree on the left.

Kade checked his film counter and squeezed off half a dozen stills of the crowd, before taking a couple of close-ups of a young man fixated on the thirty-foot-high flames shooting through the roof of the structure.

Through the viewfinder he scanned the crowd, clicking off pictures, until he spotted an officer holding a video camera. It wasn't unusual, in and of itself, but the fact that he was filming the fire and not the crowd struck Kade as odd.

He pulled the camera back up to his eye, focused on the officer and squeezed off a shot.

He lowered the camera, deciding to give the videographer some direction. The crowd was what he wanted taped, not the fire.

Kade moved toward him. "Hey. Tape the crowd."

The man looked his direction, panic in his eyes.

"Turn the camera on the crowd." By the time he made it over to the officer, he was backing up.

"Stop!"

The man bolted.

Kade pushed through the mass of people, fighting past them until he came out on the other side. He stared into the night, but the cop with the camera was gone.

"Decker?"

He turned to find Nick Brandt coming toward him. "You have a videographer out here, don't you?"

"Sure. Always do."

"Well, he ran like a bat out of Sunday school when I tried to get his attention. He was filming the fire, instead of the crowd. You need to give the man a lesson in investigative protocol."

"He's right there." Nick pointed to a cop on the other side of the crime-scene tape, and Kade's pulse kicked up. "That's not the cop I tried to talk to."

Nick's expression turned serious. "That's Rigby.

He's my senior patrol officer. He shot all the video you've seen."

Kade tried to relax, but couldn't. He'd just seen their possible arsonist, and he was wearing a uniform.

"I should have chased him down."

"What are you, bionic?"

The comment climbed under Kade's skin, reminding him he was less than whole. "I wish to hell I was. When the smoke clears…and the body count comes in…"

"I'm sorry, man." Nick hung his head, then looked up.

Kade could see the apology in his eyes. "Forget it. I'd go bionic in a heartbeat, if I thought it would have saved even one of these folks."

They exchanged a knowing look and turned toward the fire, where Fisk's crew was getting a handle on the flames.

He watched, mentally combating the blaze like an old nemesis, the angles of attack he'd use to knock the fire down to its knees, but then he felt it. A tingle at the base of his neck that worked its way over his nerves and into his brain.

He turned around, searching until his eyes trained on her face. "She's here."

"Who?" Nick turned.

"Savannah Dawson."

Kade moved toward where she stood in the street at the fringes of the crowd. He'd yelled at her last time. He wasn't proud of it, but he wanted to be sure this time. Sure she wasn't playing him, wasn't faking the trance-like state. He wanted to believe her, if for no other reason than to explain the unexplainable.

He circled her, focused on her blank stare. Her ice blue gaze fixed on the flames, unblinking. He waved a hand in front of her face, nothing.

His gaze traveled over her slender body, taking in the rigidness of her posture. There was nothing to hide the lay of her sexy black nightgown over her smooth curves. Nothing to shield the image of her body from his hungry eyes.

Tiny beads of perspiration dotted her upper chest. He swallowed, his gaze drifting to the full round swells of her breasts pressed against the silken fabric.

He slid his hand through his hair in frustration, undid the buttons on his shirt and pulled it off.

"Savannah. Wake up." He wrapped it around her shoulders, brushing her bare skin with his hand.

A jolt shot through him, taking his breath with it.

Savannah's body went rigid.

He pulled her against him before she collapsed.

"Savannah?"

She could smell smoke, smell the acrid particles in the air around her, but there was something else, something more pungent.

Death.

In one instant, consciousness grabbed her, hurling her into the moment. Only the feel of a hand against her bare back grounded her. It was a hand she knew. His hand.

Thank God he was safe. "Where are we?"

"Ogden Street. Apartment fire."

She picked up on his sadness and trained her stare on the building. "Oh, dear God!" Her knees threatened to buckle, but he kept her on her feet. "How many?"

"We don't know yet, but it's arson." He turned her to face him. She gazed into his eyes, feeling the vibes of barely contained rage pulsing in his body.

"Can you find him?"

She swallowed. "I don't know."

"I spotted a cop with a video camera earlier. He ran when I confronted him. He might be our fire starter. Try."

Savannah closed her eyes, focusing her mind and energy on her surroundings. Scanning every recess for anything about the man who'd brought so much pain and suffering to the people in the burning building, but there was nothing. Not a hint of energy left. She stilled and opened her eyes. "I'm not getting anything. He's not here."

"Are you sure?"

"Yes. There's nothing left. I picked up on desperation last time, but I'm getting nothing this time. If he's here, he's a master at hiding his emotions."

"And arsonists aren't very good at that. It's how we catch them. They have to watch."

"I'm sorry. I wish I could help."

"Me, too."

She stared at his bare chest, at the hardened span of muscle, and squelched a burst of desire, before she felt his shirt around her shoulders. "You need your shirt back."

"Keep it for now. I'm going to get my coveralls on. I'm not leaving the scene until I've gone over it."

She watched him walk away and felt her cheeks flame.

Muscle, hard and beautiful, rippled just under his skin. He'd worked hard for it, she knew. She could almost feel the determination he'd exercised with every set of reps. *He'd built his upper body to avoid building the broken body below his waist.*

The information clouded her mind with pain and she sucked in a breath to dilute its effect, but it was too late.

He stopped, turned and glared at her.

He knew. He knew she'd just delved into his private hell and she felt the wall slam into her brain, blocking her out. Warning her there were places she couldn't go. Thoughts she couldn't tap.

She looked away, humbled by the intensity of his rejection. What exactly had caused his physical injury? What had pushed him past the breaking point?

"ACCELERANT. See the burn pattern?" Kade shined the flashlight's beam onto the door of apartment number three. The splash patterns were clear.

"Lighter fluid is my guess, judging from the narrow stream between each door to facilitate a simultaneous ignition."

Savannah was tucked safely away in the car where she belonged, but an unsettled feeling still played inside him.

She'd crossed the line tonight. She'd taken a shovel to his psyche and he didn't know what to do about it. If the attack had been physical, he could have responded, countered with a fight of his own, but her mental probing was far more dangerous.

"They never had a chance." Nick straightened as a lab tech moved in for a scraping of the burn pattern material for analysis.

"Fisk said the attic was hot, ready to flash. The SOB lit it first, let it slow burn before he blocked the escape with a trail of fire."

"Sick. He had to know there would be a body count."

"Yeah. He knew, he made it happen." Kade couldn't swallow the lump in his throat as he watched the coroner enter apartment number six. "I'm going to have another look first light. Things will be more visible. I don't want to miss anything. We've got to get this guy."

"Was Savannah any help?"

He eyed Nick. "No. She didn't pick up anything." Except for his private thoughts.

"Don't give up on her abilities. She's good."

"Hey, Decker."

Kade turned at the sound of Don Watson's voice. "You got something?"

"Found the point of entry. Apartment ten. Super says it was rented last week, but the new tenants hadn't moved in yet."

"Lucky for them." Kade followed him into the apartment. He looked up at the ceiling in the back of the soot-blackened hallway where the service panel into the attic was missing. The remains of an aluminum ladder lay melted against the wall.

"Looks like he used that to climb into the attic and set the fire. Judging from the lesser extent of damage on this end of the building, he started at the other end and worked his way down. There might be some evidence up there that survived the heat and water. You got a ladder, Don?"

"Sure do. I radioed. There's a fireman bringing one up."

"Great." Kade moved aside as the fireman carried in an eight-foot ladder and pushed it into the gaping black hole before checking its stability.

"It's all yours."

For an instant, he froze. "Hold this." He handed his cane to Nick and took the flashlight from his hand.

Kade gritted his teeth and stepped onto the first rung. Each step up was more painful than the last, but a feeling of triumph laced through him as he stopped just inside the opening.

He raised the flashlight and shined the beam into the blackness.

Water dripped from the sodden roof. The air was thick with the pungent odor of creosote, a residue of slow-burning fuel that backed his theory.

Step by step, he shined the light along the ridge beam from twenty-five feet out, the limits of his light. The damage was more extensive the farther away it was from him; the closer it came to him, the less damage the fire had done. The arsonist had definitely used apartment ten to access the attic.

Kade worked his way in, focusing on the pattern of the most charring, the point of ignition, until he spotted something six feet out. "Hold on, I got something. Evidence bag."

He reached down and Don Watson put a plastic bag and a pair of tweezers in his hand. "It's six feet out, I'm going in."

Kade climbed into the attic on all fours. The timber beneath him groaned. He held his breath, praying it would hold his weight.

He crawled forward a foot at a time until he reached the object he'd spotted. Carefully, he examined the charred remains.

It looked like a bundle of paper and matches wrapped around a cigarette. Raising the camera from around his neck, he snapped a couple of shots, then picked it up with the tweezers and slid it into the bag.

It was a beginning. A link to the arsonist—now murderer—and he planned to process it to hell and back, even though he'd seen it before. In his mother's apartment.

They were dealing with the same sick individual and the incendiary evidence would prove it. But where was the link?

SAVANNAH WOKE UP the moment Kade pulled into the driveway of her house. She stifled a yawn and climbed out of the car.

"I don't suppose you locked up before you arrived on scene?"

"Not unless I'm an organized sleepwalker."

He doubted it. He'd have noticed the bulge of keys under her painted-on nightie. "Better let me go first."

He was surprised when she didn't argue with him. He followed her to the front door, noting the sway of her hips against the silken fabric. But he'd also seen the exhaustion in her eyes, the trails of soot on her face and the weight of last night's events drooping her slender shoulders.

He moved past her and entered the house, stopping in the entryway to listen.

Dead silence.

Room by room he checked the house, satisfied when he returned to the kitchen to find Savannah resting her head on the counter like a hyperactive first grader after recess.

He resisted the urge to run his hand over her back and moved in beside her.

"I felt that." She raised her head and gave him a crooked, tired smile.

"Somehow, mental stroking just doesn't do it for me. How about you jump into the shower, then get some sleep. I'll hang out for a while, then take off."

"That works." She slipped off the stool and disappeared down the hallway.

Kade made a pot of coffee and retrieved the morning newspaper off the porch. Sitting down, he pulled it out of its rubber band and stared at the front page.

The image of the apartment complex on Ogden put a knot in his stomach. The number of dead cinched it.

Seven people had lost their lives, all on the second floor, cut off from easy escape by a lunatic arsonist who didn't seem to care how heinous his crime was.

He put the paper aside and closed his eyes, his father's motto swirling in his head. *Help those who can't help themselves.* For the most part, he'd always followed his father's advice. Now he just had to get this guy before he struck again.

SAVANNAH PULLED her nightgown over her head and let it drop to the floor. Her thoughts were a jumble of leftover messages, images she couldn't reconcile and residual sadness. Some of it belonged to Kade, but most of it stemmed from exhaustion.

She turned on the shower to pull the hot water from the tank on the other end of the house and opened her bathroom drawer, taking out her tooth-brush and toothpaste.

If only she'd been able to help him last night. If only she'd been able to pick up on the energy of the arsonist, they could have tracked his location, but she'd been no help at all.

She squeezed paste onto her toothbrush and popped it into her mouth.

Steam billowed from the shower stall as the hot water arrived. She finished brushing her teeth, antic-ipating how good the heat would feel soaking into her bones. She'd sleep like a baby, and when she got up, Kade would...

She screamed and whirled around.

Etched on the glass, outlined by the moisture, was a message.

Fear pounded in her heart as she mouthed the words. BURNING FOR YOU.

Chapter Six

Kade felt Savannah's terror slam into him before the choked notes of her scream registered in his brain.

He bolted down the hall and into the master bedroom.

Wisps of steam clouded the air. He stopped short in the bathroom doorway, just as she pulled a towel from the bar and wrapped it around herself.

Desire blazed through him like a blowtorch on High. "What's going on?"

She pointed at the shower door.

Kade followed the gesture and focused on the bold letters, fingered onto the glass.

"I'm calling Brandt." He stepped closer, studying the message.

She nodded her head and wrapped the towel tighter around her, as if doing so would prevent the foreboding he could feel emanating from her.

He moved in on her and wrapped his arms around

her. A big mistake, he decided, as wave after wave of heat seared him, only to be cooled by a second glance at the message on the door. A message meant for her eyes only, he guessed.

The word BURNING leaped off the glass at him, churning his guts. "It's him, Savannah. It's our firebug. Maybe that's why you keep showing up on scene. You've got some kind of connection."

"What?" She pulled away and he missed the intensity of their contact.

"It's a message. He's burning for you. Physically burning." He watched her shudder, even though the steam had superheated the air in the bathroom.

"Did he steal my purse and keys, as well?"

"There's a good chance he did. It's how he got in. There's no forced entry. He left the table setting and this message the cops missed. He's able to watch you…"

"Stalk me, you mean?"

Caution twisted in his mind, leaving him in knots. "Yeah. We have to assume he's out there 24/7. He's a head case, but if we can find the connection he feels with you, maybe we can catch him."

"Mind games. I'm an expert. I play them with my patients every day. For their benefit, of course."

"Any patient that stands out? Have a disorder to precipitate something like this?"

"Yeah. Half my caseload has a love affair with

fire, but doctor-patient confidentiality keeps me from talking about any of them."

"Let's get forensics in here again. Maybe the guy left prints."

"HE USED COMMON vegetable oil, probably out of her own kitchen."

Kade stared at the forensic tech holding a swab. "So we have nothing."

"Sorry we missed it last night."

"Thanks." Kade left the master bedroom and headed for the kitchen where Nick Brandt was questioning Savannah.

She looked up as he entered the room and smiled.

His pulse jumped. "How's it going?" he asked, moving closer to her.

"Slow. There's nothing in here to get us anywhere near the answer. If there isn't any forensic evidence and the chats with the neighbors don't produce any leads, we're done. You've had the locks changed. There isn't much else you can do, but play it safe. Stay alert." Nick capped his pen and put it in his shirt pocket.

"Thanks." Savannah took a drink from her water glass, disappointment on her face.

He resisted the desire to touch her, to offer the comfort she needed, the physical contact he'd come to crave.

"You're welcome, but I would recommend you

take off for a couple of days. Stay with friends or relatives."

"Forget it." She shrugged. "This is my home. I'm not leaving just because someone thinks it's okay to leave messages on my shower door."

His heart rate picked up. She would be safer, and he'd feel better, if she followed Nick's advice. But he could feel her outrage building, knew she'd never consent to running away from the problem or the loony tune causing it.

"I'll move in, take the spare room. Keep an eye on her. My mom is leaving tomorrow to spend a couple of weeks with her sister Millie in Tallahassee until this arson thing cools off."

She glanced at Nick, then turned an "I can't believe this" stare on him that made him feel like an overprotective jerk.

"Okay. If it will alleviate everyone's concern, I'll do it, but I won't consent to being followed around."

"Deal, but there's already someone doing that," Kade said soberly, the words working to confirm his commitment to the job.

"Let's assume he's watching me. Why would he think I like fire?"

"Maybe because he has followed you to the scenes." Kade pulled in a breath, dissecting the information. Trying to make the pieces of the puzzle fit. If the arsonist was watching her, naturally he'd see her leave the house and follow to where she'd end up watching the flames.

"He'd assume you were there because you like fire, and he'd be motivated to start more fires for you. Keep the connection going."

Savannah's stomach lurched. The fire last night had been set for her? The thought made her sick. The loss of life, orchestrated because the arsonist believed she liked it?

She sat down on the stool next to the counter. "This is horrible. It's awful."

Kade's hand on her back sent a jolt of energy between them. Her heart raced in her chest. She searched for air and pulled in a breath.

"Let's get hold of the fire data for the last month," Kade suggested. "See if we can isolate a pattern."

She was glad he was next to her. Glad he was capable of handling the situation.

"Sure," Nick agreed.

She tried to relax, but the haunting images of last night's devastation kept zinging through her brain.

"Let it go, Savannah. There was nothing we could do for them last night, but we need to consider your patients."

She looked into Kade's face and pulled some of his strength around her heart. "I know, but I want to see the fire videos, as well. Maybe there's something in them, something we've missed."

"Okay. Whatever you want."

She knew what she wanted. She wanted his arms around her again. Wanted the current of his energy hissing through her veins. She craved the surge of desire that took hold of her every time he so much as looked at her.

Nick's cell phone rang. He pulled it from his belt and turned away to talk, leaving them alone.

"You'd better watch it, lady. You're getting too close to the flames. You might get burned."

She took the bait because she wanted to, but she could feel his resistance even though the sexual tension in the air had set them both on fire.

Looking into his face, she unleashed her feelings, raised the curtain and let him experience her torrid thoughts, each one in detail, until she saw a slight blush creep up his neck.

"Sorry about that."

"I'm not." A lazy smile pulled his mouth and she closed her eyes, but he wasn't giving up his thoughts as easily. What stopped him? What prevented him from utilizing their connection?

"About those patients." He pulled a notepad out of his shirt pocket and uncapped his pen.

Savannah swallowed her embarrassment and mentally started through the names, but she couldn't concentrate, couldn't focus.

"I can't do this. I need to pull the files. Look at their patient history. I'd hate to wrongfully suspect someone."

"I understand."

"Do you?"

Nick closed his phone and turned around. "New plan. The chief is taking some serious heat from the mayor. We're pulling together a task force and taking it downtown in two hours. Savannah, we want you in on this."

"I'm already there." A knot fisted in her stomach as she envisioned the oily message on the shower door. She was all the way in, whether she wanted to be or not.

THE BRIEFING ROOM hummed with activity as each department head took his seat at the table.

Savannah slid her chair in next to Kade's, feeling the sorrowful energy in the room.

The arsonist was responsible for seven deaths, three of them children. He had to be caught and the determination coming from everyone present was palpable.

Kade's leg brushed hers under the table, and she felt his heat hiss through her body. She pulled away and stared at her legal pad, hoping to focus her mind on the session ahead.

Police Chief Warren stood up. "Thanks for coming, everyone. As most of you know, we've had a string of arson fires in Montgomery." He moved up to a corkboard wall covered with a huge map of the city.

Pins with bright red heads, along with a series of

blue pins, had been pushed into the cork. Each pin marked the location of a fire.

Savannah's breath caught in her throat as she studied the map.

Kade must have picked up on her horror, because he touched her leg again under the table.

A neat circle of markers formed a pattern around her neighborhood.

"They seem to be contained in a three-mile area, which leads us to believe our firebug lives in proximity. He feels comfortable within this perimeter. I'm going to turn it over to Kade Decker, our arson investigator. He'll be handling the investigation and coordination of evidence. Kade."

Kade pushed his chair back, aware of everyone's eyes on him as he wrapped his hand around his cane and moved up to the board. What he wouldn't give to be whole again. His body might be less than perfect, but his mind was intact.

"As the chief mentioned, we believe some of these fires were started by the same suspect." He indicated the area on the map, pinned by red markers. "There's physical evidence linking the two red fires. The ones on Forrest Grove and Ogden. Our guy likes to build his own devices as a point of ignition. The blue pins represent the three fires that were started using accelerants alone. Tuesday's apartment fire on Ogden used a combination of both. The devices were placed in the attic, and the accelerant was used to block exits for the victims. He was looking to kill."

"Sick bastard." The comment by a cop at the end of the table was greeted by heads nodding in agreement.

"Sick is right, and it makes him very dangerous." Kade couldn't fight the concern coiling around his nerves as he glanced at Savannah, knowing there could be a link between her and the arsonist. A deadly chain that could wrap around her and jerk her away if he didn't get the answers right.

"I want the response to increase at the next blaze. Detective Brandt, if we could get some plainclothes officers in the crowd. I want every person scrutinized."

"I'll set it up."

"The fire department's response has been stellar. Keep up the good work." He nodded at Incident Commander Fisk.

"We'll be reviewing the videotapes of the scenes, looking for any repeat voyeurs. I did take a shot of a uniformed officer with a camera. When I tried to approach him, he fled on foot. We'll get his picture out to each of you, so be on the lookout."

Kade adjusted off his bad hip and leaned on his cane. "Any questions?"

"What sort of device is he using?"

"It's a slow-burning wrap. Matches around a cigarette, held in place with paper and a rubber band. Old school, but it gives him plenty of time to leave the scene. Virtually untraceable, common items. We found the charred remains of the devices at the Forrest Grove fire and the Ogden Street fire."

"Do we know what's motivating this guy?"

Kade glanced at Savannah, worried by the panic in her eyes.

"No. But there are any number of things that drive a pyro personality like his. The heinous element of last night's fire suggests his motivation has turned more sinister. Revenge arson, maybe. Officer Brandt and his team will be talking to friends and relatives of the victims to see if there were any vendettas against any of them, known enemies, etcetera."

The room stilled and Chief Warren stood up. "If there's nothing else, let's get out there and find this guy. The photo from last night will be distributed to each of you at the afternoon briefing. Keep your eyes open."

Chairs pushed back and the team filed out of the room.

Savannah stood and walked up to the board. "These fires are all around me."

Kade turned and, shoulder to shoulder, they looked at the map. "Yeah."

"The blue markers don't link with the red?"

"Nuisance fires mostly, the perpetrator used lighter fluid so the MO has to be considered."

She counted the number of blue pins as if it might ease the worry inside her mind, but it didn't. "Three?"

"Possibly four. The first one was here on Laramore. Set in a Dumpster, but the cause was undetermined. The fires on Nassau and Ruby were started in garbage cans outside of the residence. The last one, here—" he tapped a blue pin "—was on Catalpa, inside the garage. No one was home at the time."

"Did you go out on all of these fires?"

"Yes."

"Did I?" A chill moved through her body, mirroring the one she was sure had invaded Kade's body, as well.

"Yeah. The Laramore fire was the first time you were caught on film. It was my first assignment."

She watched him pull the blue pin out and replace it with a red pin. "You're assuming he set it for me?"

"I don't have anything else to go on."

She sucked in a deep breath and turned away, trying to catch a clue about the firebug heating up the city of Montgomery. "I'm going into the office today and get started on my files. It's a secure building so you can put that objection away."

"Good. The sooner we can put a name and a face together, the sooner we can extinguish this guy." Kade moved up behind her, a hairbreadth away.

"You really think it's one of my patients, don't you?"

"I'm worried about you." His breath caressed the back of her neck and set her nerves on edge. He may as well touch her—she knew how much he wanted to—but he held back.

She swallowed her disappointment and turned

toward him, heated by the intense glow in his eyes, a man on fire.

"Don't be. I'm a big girl. I can take care of myself."

He backed away and she missed the charge between them.

She could hear the shuffle of papers on the desk and turned around, unprepared for the look of disappointment on his face as he plopped a file on the table. She knew what it was, knew the wounds it would open in her heart, but she stared at the surname she'd been born with and tried to fashion a story, one a desperate fire investigator would believe.

"It came this morning."

"It was a long time ago. I was only fifteen at the time, and I never did it again."

"You did it five times. Five fires, Savannah. Five chances to destroy people's lives. What were you thinking?"

She could feel his rage build, dissipate and build again as he worked the information in his mind. All arsonists were created equal. Guilty and deserving of punishment.

She swallowed, moving toward him. "Did my juvenile file also tell you I was in the foster care system at the time?"

"Excuses won't cut it. You were responsible for your actions."

She let her head drop forward, studying the zigzag

pattern on the carpet, searching the past for something, anything he'd understand. "It was fire or my life."

She looked up into his eyes from across the table. "If I hadn't set them, I'd be dead."

His eyes narrowed in disbelief. "No one *has* to start a blaze."

"You're wrong."

He brushed his hands over his head, his frustration palpable as he focused on her.

"I was up for adoption. There was a couple that kept coming around…you have to understand, the husband gave me the creeps. And I saw things. Things in the future. Things in the past. Horrible things. I also picked up on his fear of fire. He'd narrowly escaped one as a child." Her breath caught in her lungs as the images replayed in her head.

"I couldn't let them take me. So I used his terror against him, and I started to burn. Nuisance fires. Trash cans. Weeds."

Savannah moved slowly around the table, feeling Kade's hard-edged reasoning start to soften. "I wasn't out to hurt anyone. I just wanted him to go away. To see me as too much trouble to mess with."

She had to make him understand. Accept? "Haven't you ever done something you weren't proud of to protect yourself?" She chiseled away at him, feeling the crack start, fracture and begin to open.

"I've tried to make up for it every day of my life." Her throat squeezed. "By using my profession to make amends. I've helped more people than I ever hurt. Please try to understand."

Kade stepped toward her and pulled her into his arms. She let the contact drive her memories into oblivion, choosing instead to focus on his touch, on the heat of his thoughts.

"I'm sorry the system failed you." There was no sense of doubt coming from him, at least not that she could detect.

"Go ahead and take off. Maybe I'll drop by your office later this afternoon, check on your progress. Got an address?"

"It's 1019 Garrett. Use the Columbus Street entrance. My office overlooks the back parking lot. Here's the back door security code. Come in. I'm on the third floor, right across from the stairwell. You can't miss it."

She pulled away and moved around the table to pick up her legal pad, mindful of his eyes on her as she wrote down the key code. Flattered by the hunger that burned in his body, but there was something else there, too. Something painful, something deep and dark, something she couldn't reach no matter how hard she tried.

"Careful. We have an arsonist to catch. We can't be starting fires of our own."

She smiled at him and handed him the information.

Kade Decker was dangerous, a million degrees dangerous.

"Security is on staff in your building today?"

"Yeah. I'll be fine. I'll even put 911 in my speed dial."

HE HAD TO make her understand. If he could only talk to her, make her see how good they could be together.

But what about Kade Decker?

He'd seen them together, watched the way they stood outside the flames, the way they touched as if no one else could see, but he could see.

Anger and jealousy tangled in his veins, adding strength to his hostility.

He wanted to hear it from her own lips. Watch her face for the minutest of clues. Look into her eyes as she denounced the ex-fireman who always seemed to come to her rescue.

Then he would build her a fire. A blaze to draw her closer.

A fire she wouldn't soon forget.

Chapter Seven

Savannah rocked back in her chair and swiveled it toward the window.

Ominous black thunderclouds lay in dark furrows that pressed closer to earth with each passing second. A storm was coming, spawned by the unrelenting heat.

Her mood darkened along with the late afternoon light as she turned back around and pulled another file from the stack.

It was more than a little depressing to go over all the idiosyncrasies of each one of her patients. They all needed her help. It was like a giant self-inflicted critique, and the entire experience left her feeling inadequate. Still, she'd been able to see progress in many of them, and she clung to the knowledge like a life preserver.

A brilliant flash of lightning hissed from the sky, startling her.

She turned back to the window, where a thunderclap vibrated the glass.

The storm outside her office window was violent and beautiful at the same time. Just like Kade, she decided. He was a storm on the inside, his physical pain palpable. She'd touched it, but not its source. Given time, would he tell her what had happened to him?

Another bolt of lightning streaked from the clouds as the storm came on full force. Sheets of rain pounded from the heavens as the wind whipped the trees in the parking lot below.

The light overhead flickered.

Once…twice….

It went out on the third reset.

She let out a sigh. The electricity wasn't going to come back on any time soon. She considered the limited amount of natural light coming in the large window. It wasn't enough to get through the stack of files she had left to finish.

It was time to go home. At least she had candles and a gas stove there. There would be light and a cup of tea to break the chill of the rain.

She compressed the files into a neat stack and stood up.

Another clap of thunder rattled the window. A steady stream of rain fell, sending beaded trails of water streaking down the glass.

Where was her umbrella?

Shoot. She'd left it in the car. She'd have to remember to bring it into the office next time or pick up a spare.

Savannah flipped the light switch off on her way out. It was a good thing this storm had hit on a Saturday, or she'd have had to cancel her appointments. Again.

She locked the office door and stood in the dark hallway for a moment, mentally adding a flashlight to the list.

Stepping across the corridor, she stopped at the stairwell door. She turned the knob and stepped onto the landing, glad to see the dim glow of the emergency backup lighting.

Taking the stairs carefully, she paused at the rear entrance to the building.

A shiver glided over her skin. She credited the dampness, brought on by the moisture outside. It was insidious and holed up in her bones.

Fishing in her purse she pulled out her spare car key. It would be a mad dash.

She pushed open the door and focused on her blue Ford Mustang, staring through the torrents of rain dumping from the sky. Maybe she should consider waiting it out.

A flash of white caught her attention, and she looked down at the floor where a glossy advertisement lay.

It must have fallen out of someone's newspaper. She picked it up, intent on using it.

Savannah opened the ad, pulled it over her head as a makeshift rain bonnet and bolted for the car.

The rain beat down, blinding her, as she ran for

her vehicle. She ignored the rain that soaked through the paper and drummed against her head.

She was drenched to the skin when she got to the car.

Fumbling with the wet key, she pushed it into the lock, opened the door and slid in behind the wheel before putting the key in the ignition.

Chills racked her body as she peeled globs of wet paper off her head and dropped them into the floor-board on the passenger side.

She caught her breath and smoothed the wet hair out of her eyes. The fabric of her blouse clung to her skin like cold paste. She felt like a drowned rat, probably looked like one, too.

There was probably ink from the ad on her face. She'd be a walking advertisement for broccoli, if she didn't get it off right away. She pulled the rearview mirror down to check.

Her heart stopped as she stared at the masked man in the backseat of her car, a car she was sure she'd locked. But if he'd gotten inside then he must be the one who'd stolen her keys.

A scream rattled in her throat as he lunged forward, the blade of a knife in his hand.

"Drive." His voice was low and edged with warning as he pressed the weapon against her throat, silencing her scream.

Her mind raced, panic jamming in her veins as she tried to think. She had to keep it together.

"What do you want?"

The raspy notes of a laugh ground over her nerves and pushed her terror to the forefront.

"I've got a hundred bucks in my purse. It's yours."

Silence invaded the interior of the car and drowned out the voice of reason in her head. Would he kill her now? Would he inflict unspeakable things on her?

"I said, drive!"

She turned the key in the ignition and the car came to life.

Reaching out, she flipped the windshield wipers on High and watched them frantically try to keep up with the downpour.

Running played across her thoughts, but the feel of the knife blade against her throat stopped her. It couldn't end like this...not like this.

She put the car in gear and eased forward. Fear etching terror along her nerves as she came to a stop at the parking lot entrance.

"Get on Lower Wetumpka."

She switched on her right blinker, but didn't pull out.

Lower Wetumpka was a two-lane road leading to nowhere. A nowhere she didn't want to explore, a place where civilization vanished along with houses, people and help.

"Take my cash. I won't talk to the police. You can end this right now."

"This isn't about money."

Icy fear laced around her spine and put a knot in

her stomach. Was he the arsonist? Was he her stalker? Would he be her killer, as well?

"I know you like fire, the bigger the better, but I have to know—do you go for the flames, or him?"

Fear pounded through her and she considered jumping, but she'd have to unlock the door and he would hear it before she could make a break.

"I'm not playing around. I'll cut you. Now answer the question."

He pressed the knife against her skin in measured increments until she felt the razor-sharp blade cut into her flesh.

She froze, daring to think, daring to breathe.

A trickle of blood oozed from the cut and laced down her throat. She swallowed her fear. She couldn't give in to it, wouldn't let it end her life, here…now.

"I…I don't like fire. It scares me."

"And Decker. What about him?" He relaxed the knife blade a bit, giving her time to breathe, to think. Her heart rate slowed, but her thoughts maintained a breakneck speed.

Kade…Kade was her only chance. This maniac meant business, whatever business that was. If she could get a message out…

Savannah pulled out onto Columbus Avenue, rolling the answer in her mind.

"He's investigating the arson fires in Montgomery, and I'm helping."

The air around her thickened with menace, but he didn't say anything. If she could get into his head... maybe she could figure out what he wanted.

She glanced in the rearview mirror, but she hadn't straightened it.

Identifying her abductor wasn't going to be easy. He was wearing a ski mask, and she hadn't gotten a good look at him. Nor was his voice familiar.

"Right the mirror, and keep your eyes forward."

She reached up and set the angle of the mirror, catching a glimpse of a burgundy sedan pulling into the office building parking lot from the side street.

Hope churned inside of her.

It was Kade's car. He'd come.

Right on Columbus... Right on Columbus.

Again and again, she forced the direction into Kade's mind.

Praying he'd feel her terror and follow, praying he'd trust the little voice inside his head.

Just this once.

KADE PULLED INTO the parking lot expecting to see Savannah's little blue Mustang, but it wasn't there.

Concern jittered up his spine and he felt a sudden jolt of terror.

He slammed on the brakes, and put the car in Park. Jarred by the sudden and overwhelming feeling, he watched the wipers do battle with the rain.

Where the hell was she? She hadn't called.

Maybe he should have given her a definite time, instead of a maybe.

Again, the odd sensation hit him, stronger this time and infused with a horrific image that drilled into his mind in 3D.

A knife blade. Blood. Fear.

Choking back an obscenity, he leaned toward the windshield, his heart rate over the top, his nerves frayed.

A car length in front of him, he spotted a clump of white on the asphalt.

Driven forward, he jumped out of the car and hobbled to the object. Carefully, he picked up and examined the wad of soggy paper. But it wasn't the paper that undid him; it was a single long dark hair tangled in it.

His terror ignited.

He bolted back to the car, searching for the strange string of thoughts that had been forced into his brain. Could it be? Could it really be a message? A trail of mental bread crumbs? He didn't know, but he had to follow. If he didn't and something happened to her...*left on Lower Wetumpka Road.*

"Dammit." He popped the car into Drive and slammed down on the accelerator, jetting to the parking lot exit on Columbus Avenue.

"Stay with me, baby. I'm right behind you." He whispered the message in the interior of the car, hoping by some miracle the words would reach her.

SÁVANNAH MAINTAINED a speed five miles an hour under the limit, hoping he wouldn't notice.

There were fewer and fewer houses as they drove farther and farther away from the city.

She'd been out on this road before, but she didn't know where it went, only that there were any number of secluded pull-offs. She had to embrace the knowledge that Kade might not come for her. He was a stubborn man, not too hot on believing in their connection. But she'd proven it to him, hadn't she?

She swallowed as they passed a speed limit sign.

"Pick it up," he demanded.

A shiver rippled through her as she stepped down on the accelerator, bringing the car to the posted limit.

This was no Sunday drive. There was death on the other end. She didn't know how she knew; she just knew.

She tried mentally to tap into his thought process for the answer, but she couldn't do it without breaking off contact with Kade, so she focused all her energy on him and left her abductor's thoughts alone.

Glancing down at the odometer she noted the number of miles they'd traveled and sent the information to Kade.

"Take the next road on the right."

She focused on the cat track that vanished into a dense stand of trees and her heart rate skyrocketed.

Gently, she stepped on the brake and turned onto the dirt road that had become a slippery trail in the deluge. Water filled the low spots, covering the terrain underneath.

She eased the car into the first puddle, feeling the tires spin as she gassed it up and made the other side.

If she was going to get away, it had to be soon. She couldn't let him take her any farther.

The next hole spanned the entire road. It was deep, judging by the slope of the draw it had formed in.

A plan took shape in her mind as she approached the mud hole.

Braking at the edge of the water, she put the car in Park, and quietly opened her door lock.

"We can't get through this one. It's too deep and I barely motored through the last puddle without getting stuck."

Get out of the car. Run.

He lowered the knife blade from her throat, cussing under his breath.

Now.

Savannah slid the gear shift into Drive and swung the car door open.

Raking the auto lock button as she jumped out, she slammed the door shut.

The car rolled forward with her abductor inside.

She didn't look back as she ran headlong into the woods, but she heard the car whoosh into the puddle.

Wet tree branches slapped her face, stinging her

cheeks, but she kept running, the will to survive pushing her deeper and deeper into the undergrowth.

The bang of the car door ground over her nerves, setting them on edge.

He was loose.

Panic seized her heart as she stopped for a moment behind a river oak and brushed the hair out of her eyes. *I'm alive, Kade. Hurry.*

The crack of brush and whisper of leaves echoed in the woods behind her.

Darting forward, she heard the rush of water.

A creek?

A barrier.

Fear knifed her insides.

She glanced over her shoulder and stumbled forward, her tennis shoes sliding in the sticky Alabama mud. But it was too late. Her toe made contact with a rock embedded in the muddy trail.

Unable to break her momentum, she launched forward.

The dull thud of bone on rock reverberated inside her skull.

Searing pain slammed into her forehead.

The air whooshed from her lungs. Her head spun for a moment from the impact. She regained her bearings, coming up on all fours, spitting mud and fighting for air.

She could feel the throbbing gash just below her hairline.

Rocking back onto her butt, she wiped her eyes and tried to focus, but the treetops were spinning.

Nausea grabbed her stomach.

Behind her, the sound of boots stomping through the muck sent a warning into her brain.

Panic forced her forward.

If she could make it to the stream, maybe she could slip into the water, let it carry her downstream out of his reach.

She tried to stand, but the world rocked.

Clawing the mud, she lunged forward, gaining traction as she crawled toward the stream and escape, but the feel of a boot in the middle of her back sent waves of terror crashing in on her.

He shoved her down, forcing her onto her belly.

Time stopped.

The last of her fight melted into the soil along with her hope.

She choked on the knowledge festering in her soul—she was about to die. He was too strong. He'd never let her leave this place alive.

Savannah closed her eyes and whispered Kade's name.

Chapter Eight

Through the torrential rain on the car windshield, Kade spotted Savannah's abandoned car.

He whipped off the main highway onto the muddy track.

Her mustang was lodged in the middle of a huge puddle, driver's side rear door open, wipers flapping.

Fear sliced into him as he slammed on the brakes and jumped out, cane in hand.

Talk to me, Savannah. He searched for her messages inside his head. Nothing. Was he too late?

Staring into the woods, he bolted forward. *Where are you?*

Follow the tracks. Her answer pounded in his brain as he stared at the imprint of a sneaker, a woman's size, at the leading edge of the water behind the car.

She'd gotten away. He knew it the minute he saw the imprint of a boot sole, adjacent to the open car door.

Kade gritted his teeth and charged forward, holding his cane like a club.

The tracks vanished into the dense woods, but he could still make out the impressions as he moved through the trees.

I'm here, Kade. Near the stream. He's found me. Be careful.

He listened for the sound of water and heard the rush.

Picking up the pace, he broke into a jog. Pain seared his insides, but he moved forward, determined to get to her before her abductor could do the un-thinkable….

He came to a stop, his heart hammering in his chest. Through the trees he made out the silhouette of a man, but where was Savannah?

Anger burned through him as he focused, spotting her on the ground, the man's foot on her back.

His rage exploded. He lunged forward, a bellow forced from deep in his lungs.

"Let her go, you SOB!"

The man looked up for an instant, dropped back and took off through the woods.

Kade watched him disappear into the trees. There was no way he could catch him, so he let him go.

Covering the last fifty feet, he collapsed in the mud next to her. "Savannah!"

He saw her move and his heart rate accelerated. Carefully, he helped her roll over, scanning her for injuries.

She was covered in muck from head to toe.

Blood ran from a two-inch gash in her forehead just into her hairline and a thin cut marred her neck.

He pulled her into his arms, relief spreading through him. "We'll get him. We'll get the SOB who did this. Are you all right?"

"Other than needing a serious bath, the world is still spinning, and Alabama mud has a distinctively fishy flavor."

"People pay big bucks for spa treatments like this." He brushed a lock of mud-caked hair out of her face and saw her smile, glad the humor masked his moment of utter meltdown.

"I'm calling in the cavalry." Pulling his cell phone off his belt, he dialed 911. Staring down at her, he gave their location to dispatch and closed his phone.

The rain started to let up as he held her against him again.

How had this happened? He never should have let her out of his sight. She could have been killed, all because he wasn't there.

"Stop." Her demand cut into his thoughts.

"You had no idea what this guy was capable of. He was waiting for me in my car, for crying out loud. Are you going to inspect my vehicle every time I want to go somewhere?"

"If I have to." He felt her tense up.

"There's more. He asked me if I liked the flames, or you."

Caution wound around his spine and pulled his

nerves tight. "This wasn't random. Did you lock your car in the lot this afternoon?"

"Yes. I'm not going to make the same mistake twice."

"He has to be the one who took your purse and keys…that means, he's been stalking you. He could be our guy. Our arsonist."

The information pounded deep into Savannah's brain, leaving her numb. "He could be one of my patients, but I didn't recognize the voice."

"He's familiar with you, he's been in your house. There could be a jealousy element forming."

Fear laced through her, but didn't catch her mind in its grip. "If he really is jealous of you and me, he'll become progressively more dangerous."

"Yeah. And violent, and destructive. If fire is his attention tool, we're in for a hell of a firestorm."

A shudder coursed deep in her body and broke surface.

Kade pulled her closer.

She rested against his chest, feeling the steady thud of his heart against her cheek. But try as she might, she couldn't shove the blanket of foreboding away. It kept wrapping itself around her, tighter and tighter, until she couldn't breathe. Only the reassuring feel of his arms worked to alleviate the crushing sensation.

In the distance, she heard the high-pitched whine of sirens.

Kade's cavalry was coming, but she was lost in the

moment, pulled into the feel of him next to her. She knew it then. Knew it in the depths of her soul. *He would never let her be taken again. He would defend her, even in all of his pain.*

"Stop!" It was Kade's turn to end the mind-mining. She was too close. Too damn intuitive for her own good. He put up the wall so she couldn't tap into the pool of self-doubt that bubbled just below the surface of his mind, like a contaminated drinking source. One sip could poison the entire body.

He had to clean it up if he ever wanted to draw from it again.

"DID YOU FIND anything usable?" Kade glanced at Nick Brandt then back at Savannah, who sat on the end of the gurney inside the ambulance while the medics cleaned the laceration on her forehead.

"We got a boot print. Don Watson is casting it now. We'll have to take the car downtown to the lab, go over it inch by inch. If he left a print, fibers or hair, we'll have something to go on."

"He was wearing gloves," Savannah said in a low voice, then cleared her throat and repeated the information.

"Gloves. I just remembered. Strange how things come back in pieces."

Nick stepped closer. "Anything else you remember?"

"His eyes, I think they were blue. The ski mask

covered the rest of his face, but, yeah. They were blue. And he was wearing a black sweatshirt. Hooded, I think."

"Can you describe his height and weight?"

"He wasn't very tall, maybe five foot eight to five foot eleven. Medium build, one hundred and sixty pounds."

Kade watched her close her eyes and knew she was searching for details, the kind you couldn't see.

"Anything else?" Nick asked.

Her eyes opened. "No, but I'll be sure to let you know if I remember more."

"Thanks, Savannah. You better let this bus take you in. You took a hell of a bump on your head." Nick patted her knee.

She looked at Kade and his heart beat picked up. "I'll be keeping her close. This wacko might just be getting started and if our theory proves out, he's our firebug as well."

"The chief is holding another task force meeting in the morning. Ten sharp. You'll be there to brief us on this latest development?"

"Wouldn't miss it."

"I'm putting a black-and-white outside your door, Savannah."

Kade felt her protest start, but she didn't verbalize it. "Great, we'll look for it."

The tow truck pulled in to take her car to the lab, and Nick directed his attention to the driver.

Kade climbed into the back of the ambulance and sat down on the bench.

An EMT taped a four-by-four patch of sterile gauze over the wound. "All done, but you're going to need stitches."

"Yeah." Savannah let out a breath. "Will you take me in? I'll get sick in the back of the crate."

"Sure." He climbed out of the ambulance and took her hand, helping her navigate the bumper step.

"Thanks."

"No problem." The EMT handed her a clipboard with a run sheet on it. "Sign this, please. It just says you refused transport."

She scribbled her signature and handed it back.

He tore her copy off and handed it to her. "Take care of that."

"Sure thing." She watched the EMT close the rear doors on the ambulance and go around to the driver's side.

Kade took her hand, guiding her to his car. "That's going to be one heck of a battle scar."

She liked the way he folded her hand in his. It was easy to feel safe when he touched her.

"Which hospital?"

"Take me downtown. My doctor is there. He'll pull this together with surgical glue. No scar."

Kade opened the car door for her and she climbed in. The rain had stopped. Even the clouds were receding. The storm was lifting, but not the weight on her heart. She had to tell Kade about her premonition. The nightmare she had every time she followed him to a fire.

The one that foretold his death.

"DO YOU RECOGNIZE HIM?"

Savannah focused on the blurry, still picture on the TV screen and shook her head. "No. Have you got anything clearer?"

"Let's keep scanning this stuff."

She could hear the desperation in Kade's voice. She'd been absorbing it from him all afternoon. It was time for a break. Time to relax the tension so she could rest for a minute, catch their collective breath.

"Okay. I give." He sat down across the table from her and brushed his hands over his head. "I'm sorry. I just want this so damn bad."

She slid her hand toward him, and he stared down at it for a moment before he put his hand over hers. She could feel his frustration dissolve as the contact cemented them together.

"I know. I want it, too, but it can't be expedited like this. And what good is it if we're both crazy when it's over?"

"You're right." He stood up and rolled his head from side to side. "Without clear-cut thinking, our guy's liable to walk. We have to start at the beginning, establish what his pattern is, then we can see where he's going with it."

"You missed the point, Kade."

"Did I?"

She stared at him for a long time, trying to get inside his head, but he was a wall. Impenetrable. She gave up and stood, prepared to play his game of facts only. "Okay…from the top."

He smiled, a sly grin that melted her from the inside out. He was delicious, and she wanted to taste him.

She followed him to the map, where he uncapped a white-board marker. "Our first fire was here, on Nassau." He wrote Nassau on the freestanding white board next to the map.

"What about the fire on Laramore?"

"My findings were inconclusive, so I can't rule it as arson. Fire number two was on Ruby."

He wrote it down. "Three, a residence on Catalpa. Four, my mother's apartment building on Forrest Grove, and lastly, the fire on Ogden." He wrote it down and pointed to the corresponding pin on the map.

"Was I at these fires?"

"Every last one, sweetheart."

He smiled at her and the air around them sizzled, but the mood relaxed. He capped the marker and laid it in the tray. "What's the common thread?"

Savannah could feel a headache coming on as she mentally went over the information. "These two fires are red because they were classified differently than the blue marked fires?"

"Yeah. The blue markers indicate nuisance fires.

Most of the ones clustered around you. The arsonist used an accelerant, but they were started in areas without people. We have to assume property damage was the motivation. Possibly kids experimenting."

"That makes sense, but what I want to know is why I showed up at these fires and only the ones you were at?"

"Maybe it's my magnetic personality. Maybe you just like to watch the flames."

"When did you come back to Montgomery from Chicago?"

"June the fourteenth."

Savannah stopped short. "And the fire on Laramore was the first time I showed up?"

"The first time."

"I'm drawn to you at these fires. Somehow, our connection is pulling us together, and my recurring nightmare is starting to make sense." Foreboding, dark and oppressive, squeezed her chest as the answer surfaced in her mind.

"It would seem I'm your guardian angel, because in my premonition, someone comes after you with a fire ax and he doesn't miss."

"What are you talking about?" He grasped her by the forearms, staring into her face. She could see the tension around his eyes, feel the stress in his grip. Dread pooled in her chest.

"I've been having the dream for a month. It precedes the fires. It's a premonition, Kade. I thought it was of you coming after me, but it's not...it's something much worse....

"Your death."

Chapter Nine

The shrill tones of Kade's fire pager bit into his sleep, snapping him awake. He bolted up, getting his bearings in the darkness of the unfamiliar room.

He was at Savannah's house, sleeping in her guest room, offering her the 24/7 protection she needed.

"Engine Company 19, Incident Commander Fisk, please respond to a house fire. 418 Buckingham Drive."

A knot fisted in his stomach as he dressed. The house was one block over from Savannah's place. It could be an accidental blaze. He tried the thought out, but it didn't gibe. Still, he'd investigate it as accidental until he knew better.

He pulled on his shoes, left the room and moved down the hall, stopping at Savannah's bedroom door. He knocked, but she didn't answer.

Concern jetted through him as he turned the knob, only to find her standing next to the bed.

"Savannah?"

She didn't respond, just shoved her feet into her slippers.

She was sleepwalking again. Sleepwalking to his fire. Covering him with her own brand of protection.

He entered the room, took her by the shoulders and whispered her name, until she startled awake, sagging against him.

"We've got another one. Just a block away."

Savannah shuddered despite feeling Kade's intense heat invade her body. She pushed the cobwebs out of her head and pulled on her robe, securing the belt. "I guess I'd better start sleeping in my clothes."

"I guess I'd better get this firebug caught so you don't have to sleep in anything at all." His suggestive banter sent a series of shivers along her nerve endings, and she ignored the mental image banging around in his brain.

He was still smiling when he took her arm and led her from the room.

"The call is less than two minutes old. There's a good chance we'll be the first responders."

Caution entered her mind, wisps of the nightmare still fresh in her head. "Just stay out of the house, Kade, and everything will be fine."

He didn't answer and she tapped his thoughts, realizing the request was like asking the sun not to shine or the tides to cease. Saving people was in his blood. It could lead to his death, but he knew that, had always known that.

She shrank away from the thought and followed him to his car, parked in the driveway.

"We're headed for 418 Buckingham Drive."

Savannah looked in the direction of the house on the next street over and her pulse jumped.

Smoke and flames created an eerie glow against the night sky.

She climbed into the car and they drove to the scene, but caution edged her nerves as he stopped the car and jumped out. There were no fire engines on scene, no brigade of fireman to handle the situation. Only him.

Fear worked her mind as she got out of the car. She knew the minute a woman in her pajamas ran around the side of the house and straight to Kade that he was going in.

She swallowed her fear, straightened her back and moved forward.

"My little girl! I can't find her! Oh, God, please help me find her."

The desperate mother's plea struck a chord in Savannah's heart as she stared at the blazing house, then back at him. She could feel his hesitation, the moment of truth burning inside of him.

Kade bolted forward, barely keeping his fear under control. He'd stared death in the face once. Its tendrils of blazing heat had consumed and devoured everything they touched.

Had they burned his courage, too?

He bit back the rage that suddenly filled him with helplessness and focused on the distraught mother.

"Where is she?"

"In her room, but I couldn't find her."

"Did you close the bedroom door?"

"Yes…I think so."

"Show me her window." Kade ran behind the woman around to the back of the house where she pointed to a blackened window.

He grabbed a shovel that was leaning against the side of the house next to a flower bed and smacked the glass. The window shattered, releasing a billow of smoke from the room.

He knocked the sharp edges down along the sill.

Children often hid out of fear. He pulled a bandanna out of his pocket, wet it in the outside faucet and tied it around his face, covering his nose and mouth. "What's her name?"

"Abby."

He took a deep breath and pulled himself up on the window ledge, then slipped into the black interior of the bedroom.

Kade hit the floor, down below the acrid smoke. Feeling his way around the room, he found a door. Putting his hand against it, he could feel the intense heat on the other side.

Working his way around by touch, he mentally counted the seconds before it would be too late. Too late for them both.

He heard a whimper, low and to his right. He crawled toward the sound, his heart pounding. Already the effects of the smoke were starting to cloud his mind.

"Abby? Where are you? I'm going to take you to your mommy. Abby, can you hear me?"

Kade bumped into something. Raising his hand, he felt the edge of the little girl's bed. Dropping onto his belly, he reached under and came out with a handful of fabric.

Her nightgown?

She moved, pulling away from him.

Hope roared through his system. "I'm going to get you out, right now."

Kade pulled the resistant child out from under the bed and dragged her to the window.

The heat in the room was intense, ready to flash.

He scooped her into his arms, climbed out the window, and dropped to the ground.

His lungs were on fire. Gulping air, he cleared the smoke as a couple of paramedics ran toward them.

Abby coughed and reached for her mother.

Incident Commander Fisk came around the corner of the house, waving a hose crew toward the flames. He spotted Kade and came over, helping him to his feet.

"You did good, son. Your father would be proud."

He pulled the bandanna down and nodded, noting the look of admiration in the senior fireman's eyes.

"A few more minutes, and it would have been all over." Fisk's observation sank into his brain.

He'd just saved the little girl's life. It felt good, and he let the satisfied sensation work through his whole body, realizing in the process that the endless pain in his hip was gone. Again he tried to feel it, and again he couldn't find a trace.

Looking up, he spotted Savannah over Fisk's left shoulder. "Let me know when it's safe to have a look."

"Will do." Fisk directed the hose team forward and disappeared around the end of the house to battle the blaze that now engulfed the garage.

"That was a magnificent piece of work."

He looked down into her eyes and took her hand, moving them away from the structure. "Thanks. I'd forgotten how much I love doing that."

His admission put a coy smile on her lips and he knew he'd been had, or read, as it were.

"Okay, so now you know. I lost more than a victim in my accident..." He swallowed, collecting the courage to continue. To admit verbally what he knew mentally. "I lost my nerve."

"It's back, and it's a step in the right direction."

Any step was in the right direction as long as it took him closer to her. "She was down low, under the bed, out of the smoke. I'm pretty sure I got to her in time."

"Under the bed? Oh no, why?"

"Common thing. Kids get scared in a fire and

hide. We find them in closets, under beds, in toy boxes, any place they feel protected."

"I'm glad you found her."

"Me, too." He guided her to the front of the house and over to his car. "We've got a wait on our hands. This thing really took off. The fire started near the garage. Could be our guy. Can you scan for him, see what you come up with?"

"Sure." Savannah eyed the scattering of people standing in the street. Women in robes and slippers just like her. Concerned neighbors like the kind she'd want around if her house were on fire.

Then she touched it.

Something dark.

Focusing on the energy, she tried to pinpoint its location, but he was moving, just beyond the perimeter of the house.

"What is it?"

"He's here." She turned in a full circle, stopping to face a cluster of trees on the opposite side of the street. A shiver rocked her body. She could feel his eyes on her, feel them like a caress, an obsessed touch.

Savannah swallowed. Focusing on the energy, she tried to pull out as much information as she could.

"He's across the street hiding in the bushes. If you sneak in from behind, you might be able to catch him. Maybe we'd better wait for Detective Brandt."

Adrenaline pulsed through Kade's system as he

sized up the situation. "This could be our only chance to get him."

"He's ready to run."

"Then so am I."

"But your…hip."

"We have to catch him before there are more Abbys. I'm going to rush him. When I do, I want you to get a good look at him. If he's one of your patients, we'll have something to take to Brandt."

"Okay."

Kade took several backward steps away from her and turned, focused on the bushes.

The man must have seen him coming because he jumped out of the grove and took off running.

He couldn't see Savannah behind him, but he knew she was there because he could feel her giving him the strength to run. The pain-free energy to catch the firebug.

The suspect was dressed in a black sweatshirt. Hooded. Kade recorded the details in his mind.

Savannah's abductor had been dressed much the same.

Same height, same clothing. Same guy?

He darted into some deep brush and vanished.

Kade slowed his pace, caution inching along his nerves. He almost wished he had his cane; he could use it as a weapon. As it was, he had nothing to defend himself with if the suspect was armed.

He entered the grove and stopped, letting his eyes

adjust to the darkness. He wouldn't be surprised this time. No attack from behind. He spotted a broken tree limb, two feet in length, and picked it up.

Stepping farther into the darkness he listened for the sound of movement. On his right, the brush rustled. He prepared to let loose on the bastard with the limb, but the movement ceased.

A sudden hitch in his hip locked him in place and stole his breath. This was a hell of a time to seize up.

Creeping forward, he moved the stick over the top of some brush. Nothing.

Turning in a circle, he tried to see into the dark, but it was impossible. Then he heard it—footsteps, maybe ten feet in front of him.

Kade gritted his teeth and charged forward, slamming into the shadowy figure with enough force to knock them both to the ground.

"Dammit, Decker!" Nick Brandt turned on a flashlight and shined it in his face. "This isn't the big game."

A groan sounded in Kade's throat before he could pull it back, and he sat up. "I'm sorry, man. We had him. We had the guy. Savannah dialed him in."

"Well, he must have disappeared into the dust, because he's not in here anymore."

Frustration hissed through his veins and he rubbed his face with his hands.

"I'm here to pull you off this residential. We've got a five-alarm warehouse fire downtown."

Kade's heart slammed against his ribs and he

stood up, dusting leaves and debris off his pants as he followed Nick out of the thicket. "When?"

"Started about an hour ago. The whole block, from River to 16th. Let's go."

Determination pumped in his veins. "I'm right behind you. You got an officer to leave with Savannah?"

"Yeah. I can send her home in a black-and-white."

A measure of relief spread through his body, but it couldn't completely dissolve his fear. "She could have died the other day. You know that, don't you?"

"Yeah. And she might have if you hadn't shown up. I've been meaning to ask you about that anyway. How did you find her?"

"You could say we're into each other." The focus of his answer ran toward him at a jog.

"Did you catch him?"

"He got away." Kade saw worry draw her eyebrows together and felt her fear level rise.

"We're only a block from my house."

Kade pondered his decision to send her home and reconsidered. They may have just spooked up her abductor. Maybe he'd better bring her along.

"You were going to take me home?"

"No." He turned to Nick, who smiled in an odd way. "Cancel that black-and-white. We'll bring our resident psychic along."

"No problem. See you there." Nick took off at a jog.

Kade steered her to the car in silence, feeling the

mix of frustration and fear twisting inside of her. *She had a right to be concerned. They had no idea what the wacko at large was capable of.*

"Good. I'm glad you know how I feel. Besides, I wouldn't have let the squad car take me home anyway. I'm worried about you, Kade. That's why I keep following you around in my nightgown night after fiery night. It's for your own good."

They both climbed in, and he started the engine. "I know one thing for sure. When I'm around you, my pain goes away."

"I know."

He pulled away from the curb and glanced at her. "You know?"

"I can't explain it, but when we touch, your pain rubs off on me. I feel it and it dissipates."

"Then you also know that time erases the effect."

"Yeah. You get about ten minutes out of me. Sorry."

"I'm not." He reached out and touched her hand where it lay in her lap, sucking in the tidal wave of heat and energy that flowed between them. He wanted more, more than having a woman around him. He wanted her inside of him, setting him on fire. Infused in his heart and soul, locked into his fiber. She was pretty damn close. Blood close.

If she'd picked up on his thoughts, she didn't show it. Maybe it was a good thing. He was damaged goods. She'd take one look at his broken body and run.

He pulled his hand back and put it on the steering wheel. "The entire block at River and 16th is on fire. It's a warehouse. Loss of life will be greatly diminished."

"Thank God for that. I don't think I can handle watching them bring more victims out."

Kade pulled to the side of the road and let a fire engine pass. He didn't want to see more victims either, but the possibility always existed. He maneuvered back onto the street, headed for the scene.

The telltale signs already flaring against the night sky. This was big, but was it their guy? The voyeur they'd just rustled up in the woods?

Worry knotted his stomach. If he'd used the same delayed incendiary device, he could be in two places at one time.

ACRID SMOKE permeated the night air and burned the back of Savannah's throat. Her brain couldn't comprehend what her eyes were seeing.

The shear magnitude of the fire took her breath away.

"You should have brought a thick book. We're going to be here all night."

They'd been stopped a block away from the inferno. The roar of the flames could be heard above the drone of draft pumps and diesel engines. A fine layer of ash coated Kade's car, the sidewalk and everything around them.

"This sucker is hot. It'll be a miracle if we find a shred of evidence inside once they get it put out."

"What's inside that building?"

"Storage facility for a furniture store. Do you have any idea what burning polyurethane does to your lungs?"

She shuddered. "Can't be good."

"Toxic stuff."

Savannah tried to relax, but she could feel Kade's jitters. He was dying to get out of the car and move to the front lines, be a part of the action.

Sympathy invaded her thoughts. He was like a bird with clipped wings, unable to soar physically, while mentally he was in the sky, doing what he loved to do.

"You don't think I know it when you get into my head?"

Embarrassment shot through her. "Sorry. It's hard to resist. I've never thought like a man before."

"Then you know all we think about is sex."

She found herself wondering what it would be like to have his hands all over her body, pushing her to a point of no return.

"Don't go there."

"Why not?" She looked over at him, determined to access the core of his mind for the answers she knew he was withholding.

"Forget it, Savannah."

She sobered. She was being pushy and unreasonable. His private thoughts were just that—private.

"I'm glad I've gotten through to you…"

"Look!" Excitement moved along her spine as she spotted a man in the crowd and pointed to him.

"What?" Kade followed her line of sight, and his pulse picked up. Near the back of the crowd, standing behind the barricade was a cop with a video camera.

Tension cramped his shoulders as he opened his cell phone and dialed Nick Brandt.

"Detective Brandt."

"Nick. Is Officer Rigby working this scene?"

"Yeah. He's up here on the front lines with me. Working 16th street."

"Is he the only videographer?"

"For now. I've got another officer en route."

"Our boy's over here, Nick. Back of the crowd on River. What do you say we get him this time."

"I'm coming around. I'll use the alley. Where are you parked?"

Kade rattled off their exact location and closed his phone.

His nerves were shot, but the new surge of adrenaline racing in his veins supercharged his confidence. *He could grab the guy. Sneak up from behind and have him before he could run. He had his secret weapon with him tonight.*

"What if he gets away and your hip gives out?"

He bit back frustration. She was right of course, and they couldn't let the suspect flee this time.

"I'll wait it out." He glanced at her in the reddish glow of the fire, careful to blanket his thoughts from her.

She was beautiful. Beautiful and mysterious, like no woman he'd experienced in his life. The fact that she had a freeway right through his mind added another dimension to their relationship, one he found fascinating. But how would she react if he ever let her all the way in? Let her see how scarred he really was?

He swallowed. A brief wave of regret lodged in his soul. There were physical scars as well…ugly…permanent.

Nick came up on the right hand side of the car and slipped into the backseat. "Where is he?"

Kade pointed him out. "Transfixed, I'd say. We could announce our arrival and he wouldn't notice. He's sick."

The man hadn't moved since Savannah had spotted him. It was as if he'd been welded to the spot by the heat. Video camera aimed at the wall of flame, mesmerized by the hypnotic pull of the fire in all its glory and power. A pyro's high.

Savannah's heart rate drummed in her ears as she surrendered herself to Kade's hyped-up emotions. If he didn't hurry up and catch the guy, he'd drive her crazy. She put her hand on his thigh as she listened to their plan of attack and wished them luck as they climbed out of the car.

Tension clawed through her, shredding her nerve endings. They had to catch him. Put an end to his firebug ways. Stop him from killing innocent people and messing in her life.

She lost sight of Kade in the crowd, but spotted Nick coming up from behind.

Closer…closer.

Something alerted the suspect.

He dropped the camera, scattering the crowd like a swarm of bees.

Panic scored her nerves as she tried to catch sight of Kade. Her hand went to the door handle, but she paused, driven to find a weapon. She saw Kade's cane on the backseat, grabbed it and bailed out of the car. Where was he? Why had pandemonium taken over?

For a brief moment, she saw the top of Kade's head. Then the sound of gunfire pierced her eardrums.

She froze in place, feeling for a hit. Feeling for Kade's reaction. Nothing.

Screams emitted from the crowd as the suspect scrambled out of the throng of people and took off at a dead run.

Savannah lunged forward, determination pulsing in her veins. But before she reached the edge of the crowd, Kade burst out and charged after the suspect.

Did he know the man was armed?

Fear pushed her forward as she gave chase, watching the two men race around the corner and disappear into the alley.

Her breath came in shallow gasps as the low-hanging smoke from the fire entered her lungs. She wanted to cough, but held it in.

She stopped, hugged the wall, and peered around the corner into the narrow corridor.

Through the haze she could make out a figure hunched next to a Dumpster. Deeper into the alleyway, she spotted Kade.

He'd missed the suspect.

He was walking into an ambush.

Stop! Mentally she screamed the information, but it was too late. The crack of gunfire echoed against the alley walls.

She watched in horror as Kade hit the ground and the suspect pushed away from the Dumpster.

Fear knifed into her as he bolted toward her.

She ducked back from the edge of the wall and choked up on the handle of the cane.

Listening to the frantic slap of his shoes on the asphalt for her timing, she gritted her teeth, dialed in her target and swung as hard as she could.

Smack!

The wooden rod snapped, catching the suspect in the center of his chest.

He stumbled back, wide-eyed, and fell over, dropping the gun.

Savannah lunged forward and grabbed it, pointing it at him. Her hand shook. "Stay down. Don't you move."

Nick Brandt appeared at her elbow, holding his hand against his body.

She didn't even think, just gave him the weapon and ran into the alley.

"Kade! Kade!"

Calm settled over her, induced by his mental reply to her panic. She spotted him leaning against the wall at the end of the narrow corridor.

"Did they get him?"

"Yeah. We got him."

"Nice going. How's Nick?"

She could feel his hip throbbing. He'd strayed too far outside the time limits of their connection. It might just have saved his life.

"Looks like he hurt his hand or his arm."

"I never saw that coming."

"Neither did I."

"Thanks for the warning."

"You're welcome." She moved in next to him and pulled his arm over her shoulder. She could feel his resistance. Traces of macho "can't let a girl help me" crap, but she was unprepared when he swept her to the left and pinned her to the wall with his body.

Heat engulfed her like the inferno burning next door, and she gave in to the fire.

"Kiss me, so I can walk out of here on my own two feet."

There was humor in his request, but deep in her mind and body she could feel his need, desperate and unquenchable. His manhood was at stake…his identity…his life.

In slow motion, she leaned into him, savoring the slow methodical way he stared down at her. His lips arched into a smile. Her heart flipped. Then his mouth was on hers, taking the kiss in hungry increments that turned her inside out.

Desire flowered inside her as she opened her mouth to him, tasting him with her tongue, pulling his emotions into the mix, until they parted, both winded and wanting more.

"That's some kind of pain med, doc."

She grinned and gave him a shove, regretting the loss of contact. "Get out of here."

He took her hand and they walked to the alley opening.

Did he have any idea what he was doing to her? Did he know how powerful their connection was, or how desperately she was beginning to need it, too?

She released the bothersome thought and it was quickly replaced by a fleeting sensation of eyes on them.

Cold…dark…calculating.

A shiver buzzed over her skin and she tried to relax. They'd caught the suspect, hadn't they? She'd get a good look at him. Maybe she could identify him as her abductor.

The man stood in handcuffs next to a cop car with its lights flashing. A team of medics was busy parting

Nick Brandt from his suit jacket, tie and shirt—a process he was clearly fighting.

Savannah stopped ten feet from the suspect, wishing she'd have gotten a better look at the man in the rearview mirror of her car.

He glared at her for an instant and looked away.

"I don't know. His eyes are blue, but I can't be sure it's him. That damn ski mask did too good of a job."

Kade squeezed her hand. "Relax. They'll get him down to the station. Question him. You can come in and observe. Maybe you can pick up on something."

"I hope so." She couldn't stop the fear from working its tentacles around her, or the sensation of being watched like a mouse on a cat's plate, but it had to be coming from him.

"Can we go? He's creeping me out."

"Sure. I'll take you home, you can exchange your jammies for some real clothes and we'll head for the station. It's going to be hours, if not days, before I can get into this place."

She liked the sound of that. Still, she couldn't help but feel they were under a microscope…and they were definitely the bugs.

Chapter Ten

Savannah wrapped her hands around the coffee mug, letting the warmth of the cup seep into her cool hands.

It was ninety-five degrees outside already, but she couldn't get warm, couldn't melt away the shiver that rolled through her body as she watched the interrogation from behind the two-way mirror.

Their suspect from last night wasn't going to crack, no matter how intense the questioning got. She'd picked up on his defiance and disregard for the law. To top it off, he'd just asked for a lawyer.

He wasn't one of her patients, a fact that served to alleviate some of her fear, but he hadn't given Nick and Kade any more than his name, Shane Murphy.

He still wore a replica of a patrol cop's uniform. They had him for impersonating a law enforcement officer, assault on an officer and resisting arrest, but if they didn't get somewhere fast, he'd make bail.

She stared at him, trying to get inside his head.

A chill skittered over her skin, raising goose bumps on her arms as he looked up and into the mirrored glass.

"She's watching, isn't she?"

"Who?" Brandt asked, pacing around the suspect.

Before either Nick or Kade could react, Shane Murphy was out of his chair.

He charged the glass, ramming it with his body.

Savannah jumped back, fear thumping in her veins.

"I'll get you, bitch. I'll get you for this."

Brandt wrestled him back into his chair.

Savannah tried to calm herself, circling in the tiny watch room, her nerves raw, her mind full of scattered thoughts.

Maybe the search warrant would produce something, a way to tie him to the fires and the stalking. But she'd never seen the man before last night. And now he'd threatened to get her. *What could he possibly want with her?*

"I'd like to know that myself." Kade slipped into the room, moving up behind her. His presence filled the space with energy.

She gravitated toward him. "He's not talking."

"Not the language I want to hear, but the warrant will come down in about an hour. If we can find evidence that he's been building incendiary devices, we can hold him, make a solid case."

A slice of his disappointment cut into her.

"If not…he'll be walking the streets by tomorrow." She cringed, distressed by the lack of control they had over him.

"Something like that. Maybe even by this afternoon."

She straightened her shoulders and lifted her chin. She wasn't going to let that scenario undo her. *Besides, Kade was there to look after me.*

"Glad you're so sure about that, since you were the one looking after me last night."

She sensed his admiration for an instant before it vanished behind a cloud of macho.

"Comes with the mind-meld."

"Great. So how about I set you up in the video room looking at fire-scene footage, while we search the guy's house for evidence?"

"That works. I didn't really need to go home and sleep. I can do…another four or five hours before I fall on my face."

He put his hands on her forearms, a gesture that rocked her insides. "You're a trooper, doc. I promise I'll have you home by eight tonight, hanging in your most comfy clothes, eating chocolate and sipping wine."

"Why, Mr. Decker, you're a romantic."

He grinned, showing even, white teeth, and she felt his desire ratchet up.

"I try. Anything you want to add to that list, let me know."

His lips came to mind, but she dismissed the thought.

He dropped his hands to his sides and moved to the door.

What was next? She followed him out into the corridor, masking her thoughts. If they had their firebug, the mind-meld was over. Kade would go his way; she'd go hers.

She swallowed the ache in her throat and entered the video room.

KADE EYED the handful of evidence bags and dismissed his growing doubt. If Shane Murphy was their arsonist, he'd been careful to get rid of any physical evidence linking him to the fires.

"Anything?" He glanced up from the surface of Murphy's workbench in the garage and saw Nick frown.

"Not a damn thing. This guy's meticulous, or not our guy."

Kade wanted to hold on to meticulous, but without some sort of evidence, they were screwed. He stared at the corkboard above the bench.

Article after article, documenting every fire that had scorched Montgomery in the last five months, had been posted.

"He's a drama king. Loves the flames, loves to watch, fantasize, but it's not a crime. Even though I bet we find pyromania in his background."

"Done. As an adult he's clean, but he's got a juvenile record as long as my tie. Mostly property-related."

"He's obsessed." Kade pointed at the board.

Nick moved in next to him and thumbed the newspaper cutouts, layer upon layer of them. "He goes to arraignment this afternoon. His family hired Dominic Purcell."

"Bringing in the big guns, huh? That explains why his adult record is clean. Mommy and Daddy have the bucks to make it go away. Too bad they didn't use the money to get him into therapy when he could still fight his compulsion."

"You got that right."

Don Watson came into the garage through the open lift door. "The house is clear. Anything out here?"

"Let's bag all of this. Maybe Judge Hailey will see it our way when we introduce these." Kade pointed out the clippings and stepped back to let Watson do his job.

Concern rubbed in his gut. They'd found a black hooded sweatshirt in the laundry hamper. It matched the clothing of the voyeur last night at the residential fire a block from Savannah's house and the clothing her abductor had been wearing. If they could find accelerant on it, it would be enough to hold him.

If only he'd have caught the bastard, maybe the warehouse fire could have been prevented. Hell, the chain of "if onlys" around his neck was beginning to feel like a noose and he had to loosen it before it cut off his oxygen and rendered his brain useless.

They had him now, didn't they? All they had to do was keep him.

"Hey, Decker. You're from Chicago, aren't you? Worked with the Chicago Fire Department?"

"Yeah."

"Look at this." Watson held out a clipping in his gloved hand. "Were you on it?"

The air plugged up in Kade's lungs as he stared at the picture. It had run on the front page of the *Chicago Tribune,* the morning after the fire. His fire. The night he'd watched Samantha Eldridge die and fought to join her.

"Kade? You okay, buddy?" Nick's question pulled him back into the moment.

A choked response ground in his throat and he regained his voice. "Yeah. I was on that one."

"Hell of a blaze." Watson shoved the picture into a bag.

"Took us twelve hours to cool it down and another twelve to mop up." But he hadn't been there; he'd only heard about it from his hospital bed days later, after he'd battled back from the brink of death and found himself crushed and disfigured. He hadn't been alive during those days. Hell, was he now?

"I need some air. I've got to think." He excused himself and moved out to the driveway, trying to contend with his emotions.

Seeing the picture had forced it all to come rushing back, reconstituting the images he'd tried to forget.

Flames dancing around him like living souls bent on taking him to hell.

Samantha Eldridge's body next to him on the floor, a fire victim unprotected from the heat and smoke.

The crushing weight of the beam pinning him to the ground.

Her last breath before dying while he watched helplessly, unable to keep his promise. Unable to live up to his family's motto: *Help those who can't help themselves.*

His stomach turned along with the memory. It swept him up in its grip, squeezing his chest until he thought he'd explode.

Maybe Savannah was right. He hadn't dealt with it, not yet, but the pain oozing from his bones was too intense, too volatile to touch. So he locked it inside his mind one more time.

SAVANNAH HIT REWIND again and sat back. Her eyes were scratchy, she had a headache and her body was beginning to feel the shock of no sleep.

The recorder stopped and she hit the frame-by-frame button for the fifth time, watching each face in the crowd move in slow motion until she found the face she was looking for. She paused, got up and walked to the TV screen.

Was it possible? The image wasn't the greatest, but the main features were close, close enough she couldn't ignore the possibility. She swore under her breath, wishing she could get her car back from the lab. Maybe she could have a black-and-white run her over to her office. It was the only way to know for sure. She could pop in and out, be back at the station before Kade even noticed she was gone.

She shut off the TV and went out into the corridor, looking for a ride.

SAVANNAH PUNCHED in the three-digit code and stepped through the security door at the back entrance of her office building. It was Saturday and the front entry was locked.

The door clicked shut behind her, leaving her alone in the dimly lit cubicle. She eyed the ancient freight elevator and considered taking it up to her third floor office, but the stairs were her usual MO. Besides, she needed the exercise.

Normally the place was buzzing with activity, voices echoing throughout the building, but it was the weekend and the place was quiet.

Caution hitched itself to her nerves as she stepped up the first flight of stairs, pausing on the landing.

Maybe she should have called Kade. Let him know where she was going. He would only have tried to stop her. There was a cop sitting right outside with the door code, and instructions to come looking for her in five minutes if she didn't return.

She brushed off the thought. She didn't need Kade next to her every second of every day. She'd been doing things on her own for a long time.

Raising her chin, she climbed three more stairs before pausing to listen.

Did she hear footsteps, the rhythmic shuffle of shoes on flooring? Or was it the thump of her own heartbeat?

Pushing forward, she made it to the third-floor landing and stopped.

There it was again. Footsteps. Somewhere below her.

Panic raked her nerves, driving her heart rate up. Her palms slicked as she pulled in a deep breath, determined to get a handle on her jitters.

Memories of her abduction unfolded in her mind, making it impossible to ignore the warning sensations screaming through her body.

Leaning over the railing, she peered down into the stairwell below. Nothing.

Maybe the janitorial staff was working today?

Maybe she was being paranoid.

Click!

A door somewhere snapped shut.

Savannah's heart hammered as she looked down. "Hello?" she called out, the sound of her voice echoing against the stark cement walls only to drum in her ears.

She was alone.

Truly alone.

Caution charged through her. She turned around and bolted down the stairs.

KADE TRIED TO SETTLE into the drive back to the station but his gut was in a knot. What the hell was going on? He pondered the weird feeling as he turned on Arcadia Boulevard.

There was trouble in the air. He could taste it, feel it grinding into his nerve endings like sand between his toes, minus the beach.

On a hunch, he flipped his blinker and turned onto Columbus.

She wouldn't try it, would she? She had to know how dangerous it was to go out alone. It didn't matter that they may have her abductor behind bars, for the moment.

Working his way to her office, he battled with the uneasy feeling gnawing at him. Savannah was at the station, checking out fire-scene video, just like he'd asked. Right?

He pulled into the parking lot of her building and hit the brakes.

A black-and-white unit was parked next to the rear entry and a uniformed officer was just getting out of the car.

"Shoot." What did he have to do, nail her feet to the floor? He hit the gas, pulled in behind the police unit and got out of the car.

"Can I help you?" the officer asked, giving him a suspicious once-over.

"Savannah Dawson. Is she here?"

"Yeah, and you are?"

Kade grabbed his fire department badge off his belt and flashed it. "Kade Decker, arson investigator. Is she in her office?"

"Yes. Said she needed to pick up a patient's file. Said it was an emergency."

"How long has she been up there?"

"Ten minutes. I was supposed to check on her in five, but I got a call."

Concern chased through him. "She's got a whack job stalking her. Let's get inside."

"She gave me the door code." The officer punched in the code off a piece of paper and pulled the door open.

A wave of fear washed over Kade, but he knew the emotion didn't belong to him.

He beat the officer inside, nearly colliding with Savannah in his rush.

"What's going on? You're supposed to be at the station."

She glanced behind her. "There's someone in here," she whispered. "When I called out, they wouldn't answer."

He listened for anything that might add credibility to his caution level, but it was quiet.

"You're sure?" He stared down into her face and saw the fear in her eyes. "Let's go up."

The cop pulled his pistol out of its holster and moved in front of them.

Kade took Savannah's hand as they mounted the

three flights of stairs, ending on the landing. "You can't get in here without a key code, right?"

"Yeah. They lock up the front entrance on the weekends."

They followed the officer out of the stairwell into the hallway outside of her office.

Caution worked over him as he stared at her office door, her name stenciled in bold black letters on the frosted glass. "Your office door key was on your stolen key ring?"

"Yes."

The officer raised his gun and gave Kade a nod.

He took hold of the knob. It turned in his hand.

"That's weird," Savannah whispered from behind him.

"What?"

"It's not locked."

Kade pushed the door open, prepared to let the officer take out anyone inside, but the room was empty.

He heard Savannah's sharp intake of breath and stared at the chaos.

What hadn't been broken in the reception room was scattered on the floor. A computer monitor lay with its screen smashed. Papers were strewn everywhere. The place had been trashed.

Kade paused, listening to the soft cries coming from Savannah as they trailed into the room behind the cop.

Pushing open the door to her office, he heard her suck in another breath, and anger festered in his soul.

She pushed around him, eyeing the destruction. "This can't be happening. Why would someone trash my office?"

Trashed was too mild a word he decided as he stepped into what was once a comfortable space. Her desk had been overturned along with the seating area chairs. Books lay in heaps next to bookshelves. Paperwork had been thrown around and drizzled with some kind of golden liquid.

He bent over and picked up a file folder, only to have her snatch it from his hand, stare at it and drop it on the floor. He watched her turn around, struck by the sheet of paper stuck on her backside.

"Damn." He pulled it off, stringing the sticky liquid along with it. "What is this stuff?"

She turned on him. "Honey. He poured honey on everything. All my files, patient information…everything. Even my chair. It's going to take weeks to clean this up and put things back together."

"I'm sorry." He reached for her and she folded herself into his arms. He could feel her anger at the intruder who'd spread his mischief around her office.

The officer was already on his radio reporting the break-in.

"I'll help you clean up once it's been released." He pulled in a breath as he whispered to her, catching the sweet vanilla scent of her hair as he ringed it around her ear. The contact rocked him and he pulled her closer, enjoying the feel of her body stuck to his.

Stuck to his? He pulled back, but the front of his shirt was melded with her blouse. "I don't like his sense of humor."

A smile pulled at her mouth, and she gave him a slanted grin while she tore them apart. "Neither do I, but that was pretty sweet."

He knew what was sweet, and it had nothing to do with honey.

His cell phone rang and he carefully pulled it from his belt, trying to avoid getting it sticky. "Decker."

"Kade, where are you?" Nick asked. "The briefing is about to start."

"Savannah's office. She came to retrieve a file, but the place has been ransacked."

"Well, I might know who did it. Our fire-boy Murphy made bail three hours ago. Our tracks out of court with the warrant were barely cold. Maybe he decided to make good on his threat against her this morning?"

"That's a heck of a note." He looked at Savannah, who was picking her way through the honey-covered files on the floor.

"Officer Jordan is here with us. We'll file a report and get down to the station as soon as possible."

"Hustle."

The phone went dead and he put it back on his belt. "Murphy was cut loose three hours ago. He threatened you at the station. He had time to do this."

A wave of defeat washed over Savannah. "If he did this, he did a good job. I can't find the file I'm after."

"What file?"

She looked up at Kade and pinched her honey-coated fingers together, then pulled them apart. "One of my patients. I think I saw him in several of the videos I looked at this morning, but I didn't want to condemn him without a look at his mental history."

"What's his name?"

"You know I'm not going to tell you that until I've had a chance to evaluate his condition."

"It might not matter anymore. Murphy could be our firebug and your stalker. After the lab results come in we'll know for sure."

"He's definitely a creep. Gave me the chills last night after we caught him." She remembered the sensation of being watched and staring into Murphy's eyes while they cuffed him.

"His lawyer ought to be hung for giving him your name."

"Murphy probably paid him for the information."

"Doesn't make it right." He tried to brush a strand of hair off her cheek and she realized it was stuck there when he finally gave up on it.

"I've got to take a shower and change before we go to the station."

"I'll say. We'd better get going. Nick sounded agitated."

She took one more look around her wrecked

office before she followed Kade out into the waiting room.

Officer Jordan looked up from his notepad. "CSI is on the way. They'll dust for prints. I'll talk to security, see if they saw anything. Take off. You don't want to keep Brandt waiting."

"Thanks."

"No problem." Officer Jordan went back to writing, and they left the office.

Frustration hissed through her. She hadn't found the file she was after. The name that went with the face on the video—

George Welte.

Chapter Eleven

"The preliminary evidence supports arson. We found a scrap of the device under some debris at the River and 16th Street fire. It's a miracle it survived." Kade eyed the members of the task force, letting his gaze linger on Savannah.

She'd managed to scrub the honey off her body and change her clothes in record time, but she looked exhausted.

"What did he use as an incendiary?" a cop in the back asked.

"Same old-school device we've been seeing throughout the investigation. Stick matches, around a cigarette, wrapped in paper and rubber banded together. Simple, but deadly. Lets him put distance between himself and the scene before it takes off. He's also able to cover multiple points of origin. Do we know where Shane Murphy was before the fires?"

Nick looked up from his notepad. "We're checking his alibis. Evidence from the search of his house should start filtering in tomorrow. If we find anything solid, I'll let you know."

"Thanks. Good job, everyone." Kade stood at the head of the table and waited for the members of the task force to filter out until the room was empty except for Savannah.

She looked up at him, smiled, and his worry melted for a moment. But he could feel her mind churning, working over the details of the cases, Cases with a common link

He'd put a call out to Mac Moynihan, Chicago Fire Department's lead investigator, to run the MO past him and request a file, but he hadn't heard back yet.

"Hey, shouldn't I be getting you home? I remember promising you a quiet evening. Soft jammies, sweets."

"That would be nice. I've had all the fire, mud and honey I can stand. Sounds like some sort of sick spa treatment with no benefit."

He moved up next to her, a chuckle in his throat, but he resisted the urge to pull her into his arms. "I like your sense of humor, doc. Not many women I know could put a comical spin on this."

"It's laugh or cry. There isn't any middle ground. If I'm alive and safe…it's a good day."

He brushed her hair away from her cheek, and his body charged with desire. "That was a stupid stunt you pulled today. Promise me you won't do it again."

"I promise."

"Do you think Murphy's the man who abducted you?"

"I don't know. He's about the right height. Gravelly voice. Blue eyes. He could be the one."

Frustration jolted through him, making him feel ineffective. "I've got to pull this all into a pattern. If Murphy is our arsonist and your stalker-abductor, now that we've made him, we can't be sure how he'll react. Things could get worse."

Fear flared in her eyes and bunched her face, but she quickly hid it, even though he could still feel it in her body.

"I have to get my hands on my patient file. It could still be buried in that mess, but I didn't find it in my cursory search."

Kade's muscles tightened between his shoulder blades. "I know you need to respect doctor-patient confidentiality, but you have to tell me. We can have Nick run him through the database."

"I know." She nibbled on her lower lip for a moment and he knew she was weighing her options, considering the Hippocratic oath she'd taken and the consequences of revealing confidential information.

"His name is George Welte. He's a nice man, claims I've helped him, but I remember seeing something in his file about pyromania as a young man. He's in his forties now, so I didn't delve into it. Besides, it had nothing to do with his latest relationship problems."

"Relationship problems?"

"Yeah. He has a hard time getting over his girl-friends. Gets a bit obsessive, scary obsessive."

"Restraining order obsessive?" Kade's concern inched up.

"Yeah."

"How does his height, weight and voice measure up against Shane Murphy?"

She swallowed and closed her eyes, but they popped open almost immediately. "Close. Really close, and—" she hesitated "—he drives a red car. Didn't—" She snapped her fingers several times. "My new renter…Todd Coleman. Didn't he say he saw a man in a red car the day my key ring and purse were stolen?"

"As a matter of fact, he did." Kade's pulse rate picked up and excitement coursed along his nerves. A doctor-obsessed patient relationship would explain a lot of things, like the personal connection the per-petrator felt toward her. Setting a table for two. Putting messages on the shower door for her eyes only. It was intimate. He could flip anytime, become dangerous. Dangerous enough to hurt her, to try and take her again and pick up where he left off?

His nerves pulled tight and he put up a wall to keep her out of his thoughts.

She was in danger, and the list of suspects was growing.

KADE TRAINED HIS EYES on Savannah's silhouette and watched her skirt the swimming pool nestled in her backyard, surrounded by a tall fence and lush trees.

The surface of the water was still, reflecting the glow of the full moon overhead. Warm night air, tinged with the aroma of magnolias, wafted into his nose, lending to the peaceful mood of the evening.

He could see her on the other side of the pool, where she paused next to a lounge chair and pulled the tie on her robe, slipping it off.

Kade's breath hung in his throat, his gaze transfixed on the outline of her perfect body, clad in a barely there bikini.

Moonlight accentuated her curves in sensuous waves of light, leaving the dark-covered spots to his hungry imagination.

His desire surfaced, pushing until he was crazy with need.

"Why don't you join me? You could use some R and R, too."

He bit back the answer he wanted to give her and stood up. "No trunks."

"There's a couple of pairs my dad left in the pool house. Grab one. And get me a towel while you're at it, please."

"Sure." He took a step toward the low-slung building, but pulled up short, embarrassment stopping his advance. Stopping his life.

"I'll have to pass tonight, Savannah. You take a dip. You need it. I'll get your towel."

He ducked into the pool house before she could reply, and snagged a thick beach towel off the shelf in the entry.

Dammit. How much longer could he do this? The scars on his body were affecting his brain. They'd taken on a symbiotic life of their own, and he was the willing host.

Since when had he ever been willing to give up on life? *Since he'd watched someone else slip away and been unable to do anything about it.*

He exited the pool house in time to see her spring off the diving board and plunge into the water.

She bobbed to the surface, as he settled in a patio chair, wishing the horrific images plaguing his mind would stop.

"This is great. I've been needing it. I used to swim laps every day, but once my practice boomed, I didn't have the time anymore."

He listened to her out-of-breath confession and closed his eyes.

"I don't usually swim in the dark. I should do it more often. Adds new dimension. Makes you trust what you feel, instead of what you see." She swam toward him. "Sort of a psychic thing."

He heard her slosh in the water and flip at the pool wall, swimming back toward the diving board.

Kade opened his eyes, leaned his head back and

stared at the night sky, glad for the distraction. He listened to the even rhythm of her strokes in the water, wishing he would have joined her and damn the consequences.

The sound of footsteps and rustling brush broke into his thoughts. He leaned forward in the chair, trying to pinpoint the location of the commotion.

It was coming from the other side of the pool fence.

The hair at his nape bristled; his senses went on alert. Maybe it was an opossum, looking for a late-night snack.

Something caught his eye, a flash of movement in the air high above the pool. It didn't register in his mind until the object splashed down in the water.

Kade pushed out of his chair, watching the object quiver and pulse, before it opened like a flower, emitting tiny black ribbons.

Terror drove through his heart.

"Get out, Savannah! Get out of the pool!" He grabbed the thick towel and put it around his neck.

Two dozen snakes slithered in the water, scattering like lightning in a night sky. Black racers, looking for a way out, but it was the broad black snake floating on the water's surface that shook his nerves.

A cottonmouth. Four feet of aggressive reptile, capable of killing anyone who got in its way.

Kade hobbled to the edge of the pool, his pulse racing.

He could make out Savannah's head bobbing just above the surface as she paddled closer to the far wall.

"Snakes! They're all around me!" She screamed.

He could feel her panic rising, chasing away the levelheaded thinking that was going to save her life.

"They're black racers. Nonpoisonous. Keep going, get out of the pool." He didn't have the heart to tell her the real threat was twenty feet behind her.

Kade kicked off his shoes, just as the cottonmouth caught sight of her and began his attack.

Moonlight glinted off the glassy sheen of its body, illuminating the serpentine turns propelling it closer to its prey.

Kade slipped into the pool and slapped the surface of the water with his hand, sending a sheet of water raining down on the reptile.

The commotion drew attention as streaks of black ribbon slithered in the water, feet from his body, but he kept agitating the snake-infested pool, keeping his focus on the cottonmouth.

"Hang on, sweetheart. Stay calm."

One bite and it could all be over.

She hesitated under the end of the diving board.

"Get out of the pool, Savannah!"

"I can't! They're all around me."

"You have to. Now!"

The thick-bodied reptile slowed in the water.

He thumped the surface, harder this time, as

Savannah pulled herself up onto the edge of the pool deck and came to her feet.

"Get on the diving board," he commanded, keeping his eyes on the powerful snake.

She climbed to safety.

A moment of relief coursed through him before he prepared to do battle with the cottonmouth, who'd done a one-eighty in his direction and was now covering the length of the pool in menacing sweeps, jaws open, the white interior of its mouth highlighted in the moonlight.

Kade pulled the beach towel from around his neck, praying the snake would stay on the surface where he could see it.

A black racer brushed his arm, but he held his focus, watching the cottonmouth move in.

The odds that the aggressive snake would slither off to fight another day were slim, but he held on to the hope, knowing his timing would have to be perfect. The option was poisoning and drowning, not necessarily in that order.

He looked around him. Half a dozen black racers laced through the water.

He'd toyed with the aggressive snakes as a kid. Their bite was painful and he prepared himself for the sting.

Snake skin raked his back. He fought off panic as the reptile sank its teeth into him. Then another, on his thigh. Still, he focused on the thick-bodied, poisonous snake inching closer.

Savannah lay on the end of the diving board, her lungs heaving. Below her in the water a tangle of ebony snakes twisted and turned, fighting to find their way out of the pool.

She wiped her eyes and looked for Kade, but he wasn't there.

Panic jetted through her.

"Kade!" She stood up, trying to see into the darkness. She spotted his body on the bottom of the pool. "No!" Had he been bitten? Had he drowned?

She prepared to dive in, but she saw him move, watched him kick and glide along the bottom.

He surfaced and her mind went numb.

"Are you hurt?" she yelled.

"No, but I've got one angry snake in the bag."

The beach towel sack Kade held rolled and flexed.

Savannah fought off a shiver mixed with a severe case of the willies, and watched the tangle of reptiles crawl over the pool edge and slither into the night.

Kade waded into the shallow end and up the pool steps, carrying the captured snake. He walked over to a garbage can on the patio and dropped the towel into the container before he slapped the lid on, giving it an extra whack to be sure it was secure.

Then he was there. Taking her in his arms.

A deep quake racked her body, then another. She grew hot where he touched her.

"Let's get inside."

She could only nod; she was frozen in place, her

legs unresponsive. "Give me a minute. I think I've got a case of psychogenic shock. I hate snakes."

Ignoring her reasons, he scooped her into his arms and padded across the pool deck to the sliding glass door.

She settled against him, glad for the strength he provided, not to mention being three extra feet off the ground.

"I'll get wildlife services on the phone. They can deal with him."

She studied Kade's face in the scant lighting and saw blood trickle down the side of his neck. "You've been bitten."

"Only half a dozen times."

"We need to get those bites cleaned. They're loaded with bacteria."

"You don't say."

"Are you always so casual about saving a woman's life?" She could feel his bravado flare, but it disappeared.

"So that's a yes?"

He smiled and her heart did a flip-flop.

"How many have you saved? I want details."

She felt him stiffen and his smile faded. "Let's get inside. Check you over for bites. Those little monsters are every bit as aggressive as that cottonmouth. If they were venomous, half the residents of Montgomery County would be dead."

She tried to pull in his thoughts, but the wall was up. What had she said wrong?

"I think my legs are working now. You can put me down."

He set her gently on her feet and steadied her as she wobbled slightly. "I detest those slimy creatures."

His smile returned. "I could always make the girls scream in grade school. All I had to do was tell them I had a snake and all hell would break loose."

"I'd be the girl screaming the loudest." She took his hand. "Care to wonder where those snakes came from?"

"I don't know. A prank maybe, but the cottonmouth could have killed you."

"Do you think it was the same man who abducted me? I believe he wanted to kill me. Would have if you hadn't shown up when you did."

Kade pondered her question. "If I were a betting man, I'd say yes, but it doesn't explain why his obsession with you has taken a murderous turn."

She pulled open the sliding glass door and stepped inside the house. "Jealously comes to mind. The infamous if-I-can't-have-you-no-one-else-will kind of thing. God knows, there have been too many cases of it in the media."

He closed the sliding glass door and followed her into the kitchen where she stopped him next to the island.

"Strip." She smiled and left him standing in the

middle of the room soaking wet, with a shocked look on his face.

She tiptoed down the hall, pulled open the linen closet and took out a couple of towels, then went into the bathroom for cotton balls and rubbing alcohol. When she returned to the kitchen, he hadn't budged.

"Come on. You don't think I haven't seen a man in his boxers before." Her confession was meant to be humorous, but it hadn't sparked any humor in him. In fact, she could feel his agitation grow like bamboo in a rain forest.

His T-shirt was wet and slicked to his body. She cooled a blush before it could reach her cheeks and circled him.

Blood seeped through the fabric on the back of his shirt. "One got you on the back. May I?"

"Sure, doc."

She didn't like his matter-of-fact reply, not that it wasn't warranted. She could be determined when she wanted something, too. If she had to undress him a fraction at a time, she would.

Gingerly, she lifted the wet shirt and surveyed the series of bite marks across his lower back. "The snake got you good. You need to take it off."

He grabbed the sides of his shirt and pulled it over his head, exposing the well-muscled lines of his back and torso.

Savannah swallowed a moan and uncapped the alcohol, soaking a wad of cotton. Bending over, she dabbed at the bites, sucking in a breath when he flinched. "You're going to need a tetanus shot. These could get infected." She finished and straightened. "Are there more?"

He turned on her, an odd look in his eyes. She tried to get through his mental wall, but it was too strong. She swallowed and watched him pop the button on his jeans. The zipper ground down and he peeled the wet denim off his hips.

Kade stared at Savannah's face, intent on the slightest hint of revulsion. She'd pull away once she saw the condition of his body below his belt. He braced himself for the rejection. What woman wanted a defective man? A man who bore scars. Mental and physical.

Anger burned in his soul and turned to bitterness as he shed his pants and pulled them off. Like a condemned man standing at the gallows, he stared into her ice blue eyes, dared himself to search the depths for a glimpse of her reaction, but the repulsion he'd expected wasn't there.

"Kade…" His name came out in a choked sputter, and heat rushed to her cheeks. "What…happened?" She went to her knees and reached for him, but he grabbed her wrist, forbidding the contact.

"Please," she begged.

He released her, and she felt him shudder. Carefully, she put her hand on his thigh and felt the red rippled skin. He closed his eyes and she knew he'd dropped the wall. She brushed his skin, taking in his pain.

"Ten months ago…I charged into an unstable apartment building to rescue a fire victim. Samantha Eldridge. A beam fell on us. It crushed my pelvis and pinned me down. I dropped her, and I had to watch the fire inch up, until it burned through my bunker pants…she didn't make it…out…."

Savannah absorbed his suffering, feeling the toxic mix—elements of regret, self-doubt and something else…something he wouldn't let her touch, something as raw and painful as his burned body.

He took her hand and pulled her to her feet.

"Enough." His breath came in labored puffs, his pulse pounded in his neck, but he'd shut her out. Slammed the window closed.

She circled him, finding the spot where another series of bites marred his skin, and a trail of blood oozed down the back of his leg.

Wetting a cotton ball, she doctored the bites, knowing the moment of truth was over. He'd let her into his head, but only for a second. Only long enough to live his hell for an instant. Sympathy consumed her. His experience was devastating. *Hadn't he heard of posttraumatic stress disorder? Survivor's guilt?*

"Yes. I have."

"Did you seek treatment?"

"Yes."

"And?"

"Look, Savannah." He turned on her. "I don't need a shrink. I can deal with this myself."

She stood up, considering his very male answer to the problem. "Something horrible happened to you. With some time I could help you come to terms…"

"Save it for the paying customers, doc."

Anger flared inside her. "You're too stubborn, Kade Decker, or you'd see…"

He moved in on her before she could react. Time stood still as he wrapped his arms around her swimsuit-clad body and lowered his mouth to hers.

Heat penetrated her, leeching into her limbs. Her knees threatened to buckle. She molded to him, feeling points of fire where their bare skin made contact. It was as close to making naked love as you could get, without going over, but…

She felt him harden and broke the kiss, her breath catching in her throat.

"Yeah. It still works." He whispered the confession in her ear and she tensed. Why she'd ever let the inappropriate question enter her mind she didn't know.

"I'm sorry."

"I'm not. I've felt like less than a man for too long."

"Why? There's nothing more honorable than saving human lives at the risk of your own. If we didn't have people like you, willing and able to risk everything, the world would be a very dark place."

She felt his surge of pride, but it was quickly wiped away by embarrassment.

"Are you coming at me from the angle of a psychologist, or a woman?"

"What do you think?" She put her hand on the back of his head and pulled his mouth to hers.

Again, fire flared in her body. She arched against him, willing him to let go. To give in to the desire she could feel bubbling just below the surface.

She breathed him in, memorizing the taste of his mouth, clinging to the strength she could feel untapped inside of him.

If only he would let it out. If only he would trust her…

SAVANNAH WATCHED the scenery flit past the car window and tried to relax, but she couldn't get last night's near miss off her mind. The fact that someone wanted to harm her was beyond a line of reason she could mentally cross; if it was one of her patients, it was even worse. Not even the cop car parked in front of her house last night had deterred the snake wrangler.

The gentle stroke of Kade's thumb against her cheek, pulled her back from the brink of despair.

"I know this is rough, but we're going to catch this guy. He can't run forever. He'll screw up. They always do."

"I know. I just hope we can survive until he does."

The light changed and Kade stepped on the gas. She closed her eyes for a moment, then opened them again, focused on the job she had to do. "Charlene was going to come in before eight. She's probably already halfway done with the cleanup." She thought about the sticky mess that had been made in her office and growled.

"Do that again. I like it."

She glanced over at him and pulled in a breath, then growled again, deep and low in her throat.

A slow seductive smile turned his mouth and sent shivers of desire through her body. *She'd like to bite his ear, she decided. Nibble his neck...kiss his...*

"Is it hot in here or what?" He pulled at his shirt collar, pretending to vent the heat she'd ignited in his body. "You're an animal, Savannah."

"Give it a rest, Decker. You loved it and you know it."

The air around them was charged, and she maneuvered the AC vent so it would blow directly in her face, cool her thoughts, at least to the point where he couldn't turn his infrared mind-reading beam onto them.

"Too late. I've got this mind-meld thing down."

She stared at him and smiled, resignation in her thoughts. "I know, because it's almost impossible for me to get inside your head if you don't want me there."

"You're not exactly covered in large print."

She looked away as they pulled into the parking lot of her building. "You're right. Some thoughts belong to me. Alone."

He slipped into a parking spot and shut off the car. "I'll give you that. I feel the same way."

"Good. Then we're even." She pulled the handle and climbed out. There was nothing even about the way she felt. She was losing her heart to him, one mind reading at a time, but she couldn't let him catch hold of it. Having him in her spare room night after night only made it harder.

"When are you going to reopen your office?"

He moved up next to her and grasped her elbow, a gentlemanly gesture that sent her heart rate skittering.

"Probably Friday. I've got to replace the computer equipment. I have an expert coming in to retrieve data off the hard drive. Everything has to be reinstalled. Thankfully, most of my patients were very understanding when my secretary told them about the break-in. They were willing to postpone their sessions."

She put in the security code, opened the door and they stepped inside.

"Is there any word from forensics about my office?"

"They didn't find any prints. He must have been wearing gloves. There was no forced entry, either, so we have to assume he's the one who stole your purse and keys. And he found a way around the security door."

"Maybe not." Savannah swallowed hard, realization flooding her brain. "I had the door code written down in my pocket address book. It was in my purse. If he went through everything, he could have found it."

They climbed the stairs in silence and stepped into the hallway across from her office.

The scent hit her like an overwhelming wave of perfume.

"Roses?"

Savannah pushed open the door to her reception area and stopped short.

"What's going on?" Kade leaned over her shoulder. "Holy cow."

"Cows aren't holy, they're dangerous, but what about a stampede of roses?"

"Thorny?"

She stared at vase after vase. So many there wasn't a visible piece of desk or floor space anywhere in the room.

Charlene popped her head around the door of the office. "Come in, if you can get in."

Savannah inched forward, with Kade right behind her. "What's going on?"

"They started arriving this morning at eight. They're beautiful, but it's a bit much."

"Ya think?" Savannah entered her office. It was still a shambles, but she couldn't tell for all of the flowers. "Who sent these?"

"I don't know. I haven't seen a card yet."

Kade leaned against the doorjamb, staring at the bounty of blossoms, any woman's fantasy if the floral industry had anything to do with it. But caution was growing in his veins like long stems in June. "Who's the florist, Charlene?"

"Brubaker's."

Savannah turned to him, a look of speculation on her face.

He held up his hand. "Not me."

Disappointment flashed in her eyes, turning her mouth down, and he regretted not being the culprit. He'd send her roses someday, but this was overkill of an obsessive nature.

"They're Fire and Ice, my favorite." The color drained from her face. He moved in next to her, concern stirring in his gut as their thoughts laced together into a solid thread.

"He sent them. This is a sick joke to him."

Kade pulled the cell phone off his belt and picked up a vase, dialing the number on the gold sticker, stuck to the bottom of the container.

"Brubaker's Floral. How can I help you?"

"You delivered a roomful of Fire and Ice roses to Dr. Savannah Dawson. There's no card. Can you tell me who sent them?"

"The order came by courier and was paid for in cash… Hold on, there's a message. It'll come with the last delivery."

Kade braced for the information.

"It says, 'Sorry for the mess.'"

"That's it?"

"Yes."

"What courier?"

"Atlas."

"Thanks." Kade closed his phone. "A courier brought in the order. The message said, 'Sorry for the mess.' It's his obsessive way of apologizing for trashing the place."

"Remorse is typical of some pyro personalities. In hindsight, they're truly sorry for what they've done." Savannah swallowed the lump forming in her throat and tried to focus. "Hey, Charlene. Did you come across George Welte's file in here while you were cleaning up?"

"I didn't see it, and I've already filed the W's."

A sick sensation squeezed her stomach. She'd told George Welte her favorite flower was a rose.

A Fire and Ice rose, to be exact.

Chapter Twelve

Kade's cell phone rang. He pulled it from his belt and moved into the outer office. "Decker."

Nick Brandt's voice came over the line, mixed with static.

"We need you at the Trinity Retirement Home on Sycamore. I'm here now, in the basement. There's something you have to see."

"Address?"

"1961 Sycamore—" The phone went dead.

"Hello. Nick?" Kade gave up and hung up, just as Savannah came out of her office.

"We've got to go. Brandt wants me."

"Another fire?"

"Don't know. He didn't get that far before we lost the signal, but he was in the basement of the building."

Savannah fought a pang of guilt as they left the office and jogged down the stairs. "I really should help clean up," she said, feeling a blast of heat as they pushed out into the afternoon sun and walked across the parking lot to the car.

"If you'd like, I can bring you back over later," Kade offered as he unlocked the car doors and they climbed in.

"I'll call her, find out if she needs my help. I'd probably just slow her down. She's the queen of organization."

Savannah looked in the sideview mirror as Kade pulled out of the parking lot and into traffic.

A flash of red caught her attention, and she turned in the seat to stare out the rear window just as he braked for a stoplight.

"What's up?"

"Probably nothing, but I thought I saw a red car following us."

Kade lifted his gaze to the rearview mirror, studying the cars behind them. "Let's stretch it out between lights, see if you spot it again."

She turned back around, pulled down and adjusted the visor so the mirror reflected everything behind them.

Kade pulled away from the light, his gaze flicking to the rearview. "Is that the car?"

Peering into the mirror, she saw the fire-engine red car change lanes. "Yeah. What make is it? Can you tell?"

"Mercedes, maybe."

The information squeezed the air out of her

lungs for an instant. "George Welte drives a red Mercedes."

He glanced over at her, then back at the road. "Could he have planned to get your take on the roomful of roses?"

Fear wound around her nerves. She'd never considered he could become such a threat.

"Let's make sure it's him before we do anything about it."

Her heart rate increased as Kade sped up. "We'll see if he follows us onto the freeway."

He slowed a bit and turned onto the entrance ramp. Stepping on the gas, he maneuvered the car onto I-65 and came up to speed.

Kade glanced in the mirror and saw the red car pull in behind them, three car lengths back. He couldn't get a look at the driver from this distance.

"He's behind us. Take a look. See if you recognize him."

She turned in the seat, staring at the car for several minutes before she turned back around. He could feel her frustration. "I don't know. I can't be sure."

"Relax." He reached over, laying his hand on her leg. Heat zapped him, but he didn't break contact. "You're safe right now. I'm never going to let anything happen to you."

She turned teary eyes on him and he watched her blink them away. "I'm glad you're so sure, because my life is a huge mess right now."

Sympathy pulsed in his veins as he spotted their exit ahead. "Hang in there, sweetheart. We're going to catch him."

Kade flipped on his right-hand blinker and breezed up the exit. He glanced in his mirror as the red Mercedes remained on the freeway and disappeared in traffic.

"Looks like that wasn't our guy."

"Now I feel like an idiot."

"Don't. You're smart for keeping your eyes open. It could save your life someday."

"Thanks for that."

"You're welcome." He braked at the light and turned onto Sycamore, spotting a single fire engine in front of the Trinity Retirement Home. Whatever was going on, it wasn't a serious fire; the response was minimal.

He pulled into the parking lot, easing through groups of elderly people, some in wheelchairs, others seated in folding chairs.

"Looks like they got the place evacuated." He pulled into a parking space next to where Nick Brandt and IC Fisk stood. They both looked up at the same time.

Kade and Savannah climbed out of the car.

"Decker." Fisk nodded. "Your guy's at it again."

"I don't see any smoke."

"That's because a maintenance worker smelled it before all hell broke loose. Seems he's always catching the residents down there lighting up. He entered the room and found three devices that had just ignited in a pile of rags. He hit them with an extinguisher."

Brandt shook his head. "It could have leveled the entire building if the O_2 tanks would have blown."

Caution worked through Kade's body, making him as tense as a racehorse in the starting gate. "What did he use?"

"Cigarette, wrapped with matches and paper. Tied up pretty in a rubber band," Brandt said.

"That sounds like our guy. Let's have a look."

He put his hand on the small of Savannah's back, guiding her forward, and keeping stride with Nick and Fisk as they entered the deserted nursing home and made their way into the basement, pausing next to a door crisscrossed with crime-scene tape.

"Any chance they have a security camera?" Kade asked, hope churning his insides.

"Yeah. One at every exit. We're in the process of acquiring the tapes."

"Great. We can pinpoint the timetable to within half an hour. The incendiary takes between five and ten minutes to ignite. If we're lucky, we caught a shot of his ugly mug when he came in and when he left." Kade reached for the doorknob into the room.

"Stop!" A warning, sharp and menacing, stabbed into Savannah, taking her breath with it. She stepped back and slumped against the wall in the cement corridor.

"You can't go in there."

Concern pulled Kade's brows together and he grasped her elbow. "You got something?"

Fisk and Brandt were staring at her now, but she closed her eyes anyway, trying to find a trace of the dark energy that had swept over her when Kade touched the knob.

Images flashed in her mind's eye, a premonition, fiery and ominous. "We have to get out of here. Now!"

She backed down the hall, terror pulsing in her body. She could barely keep it under control. "There's a secondary device." She could see the timer in her head, see the seconds ticking off the clock.

"He's planted a bomb!"

"Move! Everyone move." Kade grabbed her arm, steering her toward the exit.

She could feel his dread stacking on top of her own as he jerked open the stairwell door.

Brandt and Fisk were right behind them. Fisk's frantic voice on his radio drummed in her ears as he ordered his crews to push the evacuees farther back.

Kade pulled her up two flights of stairs and out into the corridor.

"How much time is left."

"None." Fear shook her.

"Run!" Kade bolted forward, his focus on the front entrance of the building.

They hit the glass doors and raced through.

"Get down. Everyone get down!" He pulled Savannah to the right and they hit the dirt.

A low rumble shook the building.

He covered her with his body as the percussion

from the blast blew through the building, shattering the windows in its explosive rampage.

Shards of glass and debris rained down. People screamed in terror and pain. Hell had officially broken loose.

Kade raised his head, surveying the damage. There were injured. Residents who were too weak or too immobile to run.

Columns of black smoke rolled out the windows where glass used to be.

Fisk was already on his radio, calling in the cavalry.

Brandt was on his cell phone, doing the same.

Kade put his head back down, burying his face in Savannah's hair. Listening for her breath, feeling for movement. She'd just saved their lives.

She moved next to him, and he backed off so she could roll over. "That was close."

He smoothed the hair out of her eyes and stared at her lips. "You got that right, darlin'. It looks like our guy has stepped it up. If this nursing home's evacuation protocol hadn't been followed…"

Savannah shuddered, caught up in images that tumbled in her head and turned her stomach, making her feel sick inside. "Let's get moving. See if we can help these folks. I've had some emergency medical training."

He helped her sit up, then stand, flicking glass off her clothes. "Are you okay?"

"Yeah. You make a great shield." She stared up

into his face, caught off guard by the tenderness in his eyes. She swallowed and looked away. "Come on. I'm fine."

They waded into the chaos at the far end of the parking lot. The seniors had sufferered mostly cuts from flying glass and debris.

Sirens wailed. The blast from a fire engine air horn preceded the vehicle pulling into the parking lot, followed by two more engine companies.

Kade disappeared into the crowd and returned with a first aid kit. "It's not much, but it's all I have."

Savannah unzipped the kit and grabbed a handful of gauze pads before easing into the sea of injured nursing home patients.

They all seemed dazed, lost in the confusion that permeated the air along with the smell of smoke. She did the best she could, giving those with deep lacerations a four-by-four bandage and showing them how to apply direct pressure to the wound before moving on to the next victim.

Relief spread through her ten minutes later, when a mass-casualties unit pulled into the parking lot with its lights flashing, followed by a string of ambulances.

"Great job, doc," Kade whispered over her left shoulder.

She turned around, needing his arms around her to mitigate the horror she could feel saturating her senses.

"No one died today, Savannah. It's a good day."

He smiled down at her and she melted against him, pulling his optimism into her veins.

"You're right," she whispered, listening to the steady beat of his heart under her cheek.

He cradled her head in his hand as he held her next to him, sharing in the slow letdown of emotion that zinged between them.

Desire stirred in her body, replacing the despair and helplessness she'd felt only moments ago.

That's when it hit her.

The feeling of being watched, the overwhelming sensation of disapproval, anger and something darker....

Hatred.

A chill skittered over her skin.

"What is it?"

"He's here."

Kade continued to hold Savannah, scanning the scene over the top of her head. "I'm not seeing Murphy, and I don't know what Welte looks like."

The tendrils of information, which moments ago had been so strong, weakened and dissipated.

"He's gone. He must have been driving by." She turned toward the road, staring at the string of cars slowing down to get a look at the fire.

A block up the street from the nursing home, she saw a red Mercedes pull into the turning lane.

"There."

Kade followed her line of sight. "Welte?"

"It looks like his coupe, but there's no way to know for sure. There are probably hundreds of them in the city."

"Take it easy. We'll get Brandt on it."

She leaned into him again, suddenly exhausted. How much more could they take before the flames brought her premonition to life?

The sensation of impending danger—and death— wrapped around her thoughts.

She knew it was coming, could feel it in her bones.

"His MO HAS CHANGED?" an officer at the far end of the table asked.

"Yeah. It looks that way, but we know it's our guy, because of the signature incendiary device. Incident Commander Fisk and Detective Brandt got a good look at them before the explosion. It appears he was after a sizable body count this time, and he would have gotten it if the devices hadn't been discovered by an alert maintenance worker and extinguished. Unfortunately, the videotapes from the security cameras were destroyed in the fire."

He directed his focus on Nick. "Any info on Shane Murphy's alibis for the other fires?"

"Every one of them checked out and he hasn't shown up on-scene since the River Street blaze. The evidence against him doesn't support anything more than a fascination with fire. We got nothing."

Disappointment washed over his hopes, dashing

them. If the list of suspects dwindled any further, they'd be staring at a dead end.

"Any questions?" He glanced around the table, where the subdued task force members prepared to exit the room.

He didn't blame them for feeling dejected. He was damn near there himself. Yesterday's nursing home fire had brought them all to their knees, and the lack of suspects would keep them there.

Kade winked at Savannah as she got up to stretch her legs and caught up with Nick before he could take off. "You run George Welte?"

"Yeah. Nothing recent. He has some pyromania in his juvenile file, but that's it."

"You got a plate number on his red Mercedes?"

"Yeah."

Kade grabbed a notepad and pen and copied the number down. "If we spot his vehicle, we'll be able to verify his identity for certain. Thanks."

"No problem." Nick Brandt left the room, closing the door behind him.

Kade moved up next to Savannah, who studied the fire map. He could feel her frustration and it blended with his own. "I think we should go after Welte."

She turned toward him. "If you must, but I have to tell you, I've never picked up on the kind of vengeful thoughts that I caught yesterday at the fire. He doesn't have it going on."

"You have to admit, he's involved somehow."

"Yes, but how?"

Kade glanced at the map. "If we could establish a pattern, maybe we could come up with an answer. The frequency is escalating. This arsonist is trying to make a statement, tell us something."

He picked up a marker and strode to the whiteboard. "If we cut out the nuisance-type fires and concentrate on the more destructive fires—" he wrote Forrest Grove on the white board "—maybe we can find something to tie them together, besides the same incendiary."

Under it, he scribbled Ogden, then River Street, followed by Sycamore.

"Four big blazes, one common device."

"We were both at every blaze." She walked to the other side of the room, arms crossed, pacing as she stared at the floor.

He could feel her working the facts. Massaging them into some form of understanding, some sort of consistency they could work with.

Savannah's head throbbed as she stopped and stared at the white board until the letters blurred. She blinked, recognition coursing through her veins as she brushed past Kade and approached the board.

"Look at this." She picked up a marker and uncapped it. "If you take the first letter of each street name." She circled each capital letter straight down in a row and stepped back.

Fear knotted in her stomach and she stared at the obvious, the pattern they'd somehow missed.

He turned to her, pulling her into his arms, feeling her terror and marrying it with his own.

The line of letters spelled out the arsonist's motive. FOR S. If their next big fire started on a street beginning with the letter A, it would give weight to the dread squeezing inside his chest.

Savannah Dawson was the target, he was setting fires and burning Montgomery down, FOR SAVANNAH.

HOW COULD SHE? How could she enjoy the flames with another man?

He pushed a pin into the photograph, securing it to the wall. Hadn't he shown her how much he cared? How far he would go for her? He stared at the picture of them together amidst a sea of elderly people.

Anger dragged him close to tears.

He blinked hard and focused on the wall. Reaching out, he trailed his finger down the line of appointment cards, each one representing a date.

A date with the woman he loved, but she'd betrayed him. He could see it in the pictures on the wall, in the man who always seemed to be touching her somehow, always by her side. Kade Decker protected her, kept her just out of his reach.

His throat squeezed shut and he tried to fight the compulsion eating through his reasoning like acid, but it was too strong.

She liked fire didn't she? He'd been so sure.

On Fire

He'd burned for her, but maybe just fire wasn't enough.

Maybe her love required more, a bigger, better sacrifice.

A human sacrifice.

Chapter Thirteen

Kade listened to the address being sent over his fire pager and bit back rage. He didn't want it to be true, but it was.

"Engine Company 10, Ladder Company 19, IC Fisk, please respond to an apartment fire, 1501 Amity."

The second letter in Savannah's name. His nerves twisted around the information as he pulled on his clothes and headed down the hall to her room to wake her. But she was already up, standing next to the window, fully dressed.

"Savannah?"

She turned toward him, and he saw the glistening trails of tears on her cheeks. "Come here."

Kade pulled her into his arms, feeling the tension in her body, sucking her fear into his soul, wrapping it in logic and sending it back out to her. "It's not your fault. This guy is on some kind of a rampage we don't understand."

"I know, but I can't help feeling responsible. If it's

George Welte, I should have seen it. I should have headed it off."

"No one made him do this. We always have a choice." He felt her relax and knew his reasoning had gotten through. Whether or not it would stick was another story.

"We've got to roll. A fire on Amity."

"It fits the pattern."

"Yeah, afraid so." He took her hand and led her out of the room. "With his pattern established, we can second-guess him. Catch him. We'll get Brandt to go after a warrant. If he's picking targets off a map in the comfort of his own home, it's enough to nail him."

The end was near. He didn't know how he knew; he just did. But it was the dark shadow hanging over his heart that worried him.

Would he be around when it was all over?

Not if Savannah's premonition held true.

SAVANNAH TRIED to relax as she stood next to the car.

The building on Amity was a total loss, but by some miracle all of the residents had made it out alive, despite their front doors having been doused with lighter fluid.

It was their guy…their maniac.

She watched Kade stride toward her. He looked exhausted. Dark circles tinted the skin under his eyes. A hint of stubble covered his handsome face. She knew he'd spent plenty of time beating himself up over this investigation, but she was glad to see him without his cane. It was one less drag on his soul.

He'd been using it less and less. His pain had subsided substantially since they'd first touched all those weeks ago.

He glanced up and she felt his mental once-over like a lover's touch.

Dropping her gaze she stared at the ground, circling the pavement with her toe. It was true he'd used her in the beginning, but he was changing a degree at a time, and she dared to hold on to hope.

"Ready to go?" he asked, a slight smile on his lips.

"Yeah. You look beat."

"It's nothing eight hours won't cure."

She'd like to do eight hours with him…in her bed.

Kade tried to keep his thoughts under control as Savannah's heated desires slammed into his brain, sapping his willpower. He forced up a mental wall to keep her out. He wanted more than the physical satisfaction of making love to her.

He stood against a wave of emotion that washed over him and squelched it with reality. His reality. He was damaged goods; no matter how hard he tried to convince himself she wouldn't mind, in his soul it just didn't gibe.

"Let's get you home. It's 1:00 a.m. and I've done all I can do here tonight."

He took her elbow, steering her to the car, hoping she'd go quietly and leave him in his private hell.

IT WAS HOT.

Scorching.

Savannah tried to move but couldn't.

The back of her throat burned. Her terrified screams trapped behind a piece of duct tape over her mouth.

Everywhere there were flames, rolling like red-orange demons in twisted movement. Flicking close, pulling back, taunting her to join them in their devilish dance.

She closed her eyes trying to focus. She was tied up.

Rolling onto her back, she stared at the ceiling, at the man who leaned over her, his eyes cobalt blue, a hole where his heart should be.

Terror rushed into her body. She thrashed on the floor like a fish stranded on the rocks, stilling as she looked past the flames and into Kade's eyes.

The madman next to her vanished, reappearing behind Kade.

She watched him raise the fire ax over Kade's head.

Her heart slammed against her ribs.

"Run!" she tried to scream. "Run!"

A hand grasped her shoulder. She rolled away from him, but he continued to shake her.

His voice low, familiar.

"Savannah, wake up. We've got to go."

The last remainder of sleep left her and she catapulted awake. She bolted up in bed, her breath coming in heavy gulps, her skin buzzing.

"A nightmare?"

She stroked her bare arms. "Yes. One that's getting more vivid each time. The closer you get to…"

"Come here." He sat down on the edge of the bed and pulled her into his arms.

She leaned into him. "Tell me you'll be careful, stay out of burning buildings."

"Not a problem. It's going to be a while before they let me suit up again."

"Promise?" She pushed back from him, staring into his face. She wasn't beyond begging. On her knees if she had to. The horrific vision would never transpire if he'd stay out of the fire.

"Cross my heart." He put an X on his chest, but the lighthearted gesture couldn't dispel the slow, creeping terror that latched on to her mind.

"Now throw on some clothes. We've got to get out of here."

He left her alone. She slipped into a pair of jeans and a T-shirt, donned her tennis shoes and met him in the kitchen.

He held up his hand as a dispatcher's voice came over the pager, repeating the location of the fire.

"Come on. It's a duplex on Weston, less than a mile from here. It's fully involved."

Concern stirred in her blood stream as she followed Kade out the door to the car.

"Is it occupied?"

"I'm afraid so."

She couldn't stop her stomach from squeezing or

her heart from pounding. No more. No more lives lost, no more death; she couldn't stand it.

If she had to walk up to every spectator and stare him down, she would. Every vibe would be hers for the taking.

They climbed in. Kade fired the engine and put the car in Drive, his mind racing as he stepped on the gas and pulled away from the curb.

"This street name doesn't fit the pattern. Maybe we were wrong. Maybe there is no pattern, just a lunatic who doesn't care where he burns down lives and property."

Savannah was tense. He could feel her tension in his body. Knew her mind was turning over every possible angle. But there was something else tonight. A level of determination he hadn't felt in her before. She wanted this guy as much as he did, and she was willing to do anything to get him. That's what scared him the most.

This arsonist was dangerous, unpredictable. One minute he wanted to kill her, the next he was sending roses to smooth over the bumps.

Caution spread over him and he put up a wall to keep her out.

Did she know how much he cared about her?

His heart squeezed in his chest, but he pushed the emotions away. Once they caught this firebug, it was over. She'd never want a cripple around to slow her down. He wasn't even sure if he trusted the counter-productive feeling stewing in his mind and body.

Touching her afforded him a reprieve from his pain. She'd believe that was the only reason he wanted her.

Kade spotted a column of smoke reaching into the night sky and prepared himself. He'd never get used to being the Johnny-come-lately. It didn't sit well in his mind or his gut, and the knowledge added to his self-doubt. Would he ever be whole again?

Her hands on him had certainly made him feel like a man, but he couldn't be sure of her thoughts. Didn't trust the lust he'd seen burning in her eyes. He swallowed his doubts and turned onto Weston, pulling to a stop behind a line of fire engines.

"It looks bad." She stared at him, her ice blue eyes wide in the glow of the flames. "I hope they got out."

"Me, too. Sit tight." He climbed out of the car and spotted Fisk, his head bowed as he listened to the fireman standing next to him.

Kade headed in his direction.

Savannah slumped in the seat. There were victims this time; she'd known it the minute they pulled up on scene and their energy engulfed her.

She let out a sigh as a fresh wave of remorse plowed over her and sucked her under. She held her breath, watching Kade through the front windshield as Fisk gave him the news.

His shoulders slumped. She felt the dark weight settle over him like a cloak.

She had to help. If this was an arson fire and their

arsonist was behind it, maybe she could find him. She had to try.

Reaching for the door handle, she climbed out of the car, shut the door and leaned against it. She closed her eyes, sucking in the myriad of energy that swirled around her and sent echoes into her head.

Snippets of feeling, traces of leftover emotion, clips of movement strung together like an old movie. Even sound bites of conversations long past.

She began to sort through it, discarding the weakest elements.

Pushing away from the car, she opened her eyes and stared into the night.

He was here, watching. Watching like he always did. Watching because she was watching, because he believed she liked it.

A chill rippled over her skin as she turned, trying to pinpoint his exact location.

There were a lot of lost souls out tonight. One behind every bush. She blocked out their emotions, closed her mind to their perverted deeds.

They were here for the flames. Here to watch, to fantasize, to feed their need on the fire's energy.

Her heart rate picked up as she completed the circle and honed in on one individual.

He hung on the edges of the crowd, a video camera in his hand pointed at the flames.

Shane Murphy.

She felt Kade's eyes on her. She looked up, let the

information pass between them and pointed in Murphy's direction.

The chase was on; she knew it the moment Kade lunged forward. Fear seized her insides. Murphy had been armed the last time he was confronted.

Panic engulfed her as she looked around, spotting Detective Nick Brandt just getting out of his car.

"Nick!" She ran to him. "It's Murphy again. Kade took off after him, headed down the street."

"West?"

"Yeah."

Nick unholstered his gun and jogged into the night.

She listened until she could no longer hear the slap of his shoes on the asphalt before walking back to the car, filtering for Kade's thoughts, praying he wouldn't do anything crazy.

A chill skittered over her skin, a warning mixed with emotion.

She stopped short, trying to isolate the source.

Close. Someone was close. She could feel the intensity of their obsession. Dark and light mixed. Legitimate and unreasonable.

She swallowed her fear and moved closer to the car.

Had Shane Murphy doubled back? Casually she scanned her surroundings, even as the feeling of being watched intensified.

She resisted the urge to get into the car and lock the doors. Instead, she reached into the car and picked up Kade's cane off the seat.

The hair at her nape bristled as she focused on an alcove of brush. Tension knotted her muscles, but she pressed forward, moving slowly toward the voyeur's position.

She was picking up on his emotions in rapid-fire detail.

Nervous. Awkward. Embarrassed. Sorry.

Sorry?

Caution wound tightly around her nerves as she inched closer to his hiding place. If he was feeling remorse for what he'd done, then there had to be guilt.

The thought crystalized in her mind along with hesitation. She couldn't let him slip away, but it was stupid to try to apprehend him herself.

She analyzed his tangle of emotions. He was ready to bolt. She'd simply have to follow him if he left the scene; then she could give the information to Detective Brandt.

The brush behind her rattled, leaves rustled against one another.

Her heart pounded in her ears as she turned around.

A dark shape moved less than twenty feet away, headed in the opposite direction.

Savannah glanced over her shoulder just in time to see Kade stride out of the shadows. She couldn't wait for him. She couldn't risk letting the arsonist vanish into the night without getting a look at him.

Mentally she begged Kade to follow and moved into the pattern of shadows that lined the street, keeping to the fringes, staying far enough back that he wouldn't know she was following him.

She filed the details of his appearance each time he passed under a streetlight. Medium height, slight build, dark clothes, sandy blond hair.

He stopped and turned in her direction, pulled the hood of his sweatshirt up over his head and started moving again.

Savannah tried to blend in with the shrubbery, adding one more detail to her list. He wore glasses.

An instant of recognition flared in her mind, but she kept moving as she listened for Kade, hearing the distinct rhythm of his footsteps behind her and to the right.

His nearness gave her new courage. She picked up her pace, rounded the corner onto Fillmore Street and stopped.

She stepped behind a magnolia tree and peeked out. A lump forming in her throat as she watched George Welte climb into his red Mercedes and pull away from the curb without turning on his lights.

Savannah leaned against the tree, wrestling with the information. It made perfect sense. He was the one who put the message on the shower door and arranged the place settings. He'd been setting the fires for her, living with his ecstasy and his remorse like some kind of on-off switch. He'd abducted her, slammed her into a swim party with his slimy friends, then sent her a roomful of roses.

Why?

"Why is right."

She jumped as Kade moved up behind her. "It's George Welte."

He slipped his arms around her and she leaned into him.

"Did you get Murphy?"

"Yeah. They're taking him in now."

"Good. But George was here and he was doing more than watching." She stepped back. "He may have set this fire."

"You're sure?"

"I picked up on his remorse."

"I'll talk to Nick. See if we can get a search warrant tonight. It's a good thing he didn't make you."

"I suppose you're right."

They turned around, headed for the fire scene.

Nick Brandt greeted them as they approached. "Where have you been?"

"Chasing down a lead, but this one's for real. A patient of Dr. Dawson's. George Welte. He was here tonight. Watching. Savannah seems to think he set this fire."

"That so?"

"Yes."

"Can you give me a description?" Nick asked.

"Medium height, slight build. He had blond hair and wore jeans. Dark hooded sweatshirt. The kicker is I followed him and he climbed into his red Mercedes. It was George Welte. No question."

"There was an eyewitness across the street. Your descriptions match and she saw him near the garbage cans just before the fire started."

"We've got probable cause. We'll get a search warrant. If he did this, he's facing two counts of murder."

Savannah's stomach fisted. Being sorry wasn't going to be enough. He'd have to face justice.

"The homeowners, Maude and Denton Lundy, didn't make it out."

Her heart sagged. *If only she'd have found his file, maybe she could have prevented this.*

Kade put his arm around her. "Don't go there. You had no way of knowing what this guy was capable of unless he told you outright. If he's our man, we'll have the evidence to prove it. He won't ever do it again."

She pulled strength from him and nodded, hoping it would all end tonight. Hoping the flames would finally be extinguished, but praying Kade would... *Stay.*

The last thought hung up in her head and pounded around in her brain. She tried to pull it back from him, but it was too late.

She felt his arm tighten at her waist, but couldn't look up into his face. There was no getting into his mind for the answer; she'd already tried.

He was intentionally keeping her out. Protecting

his thoughts like he protected his injury, his post-traumatic stress disorder and his heart. But she wouldn't give up…she couldn't give up.

KADE RAISED his camera and squeezed off a shot, re-focused and squeezed off another one. "Point of origin." He stepped back, lowered the camera and pointed to the twin metal trash cans, at least what was left of them.

"The fire was not inside these, it got into the garage wall on fire and the rest is history."

He gave Savannah a glance and moved around into the garage, clicking off several snapshots of the interior walls, to the ceiling where the fire had burned into the attic. "Just like the house on Buckingham Street. Same MO. Accelerant in the garbage cans. Meant to be a nuisance fire, but it got out of hand."

"Is Nick heading for Welte's place?" Savannah asked.

"As soon as he secures a warrant."

She wandered out of the charred garage and he trailed after her, caught up in her dark mood.

He'd been in the same boat too many times over the past several months. He let his camera drop on the end of its neck band and grasped her shoulders.

"Come on. It's over. He's as good as gone."

"I know, but I can't let go of knowing that I may have been able to prevent this from happening. It makes me wonder about my ability to rehabilitate these people. It points out the flaws in my thinking. I thought I could save the world…."

"But you found out you're only human? You're only bound to use the information you have and even with your gift you can't predict what someone might do?"

"Something like that."

He brushed his fingers along her cheek, feeling a charge enter his body. He sucked it in, wanting more…wanting so much more. He ground his teeth together and stepped back. He'd used her. He wasn't proud of it, but somewhere along the way usage had turned to need, need to desire…desire to—

"We've got it!" Nick Brandt waved a piece of paper as he climbed out of his car. "Judge Hailey wasn't happy about jumping out of bed at 2:00 a.m., but he gave us the warrant."

Kade felt Savannah's tension escalate.

"His residence is on Palmeri Drive. Follow me."

He took her hand as they raced down the driveway to the car, climbed in and pulled in behind Detective Brandt.

Kade could feel the excitement in the air. He was having a hard time controlling his own, as evidenced when he glanced down at the speedometer and backed off the gas pedal. A cool head would prevail, maybe, if he didn't rear-end his buddy in the race for the truth.

"We'll have to stay back. Give Brandt space to do his job before we get a look at the evidence."

"I know."

Was she upset?

"Yes, I'm upset. I'm glad we're going to get him, but I'm confounded by his Dr. Jekyll-Mr. Hyde, reality. The man who abducted me was evil right down to his rotten soul. He took sick delight in what he planned to do to me. I never got that from George."

Caution sluiced in his veins. "Don't get ahead of this thing. Let's have a look first. See what the evidence has to say."

"You're right. I just need to settle down, let things happen, then make my decision based on the facts."

"There you go." He knew she'd found a measure of acceptance in his words because the tension dissipated.

They turned onto Palmeri Drive and he braked behind Brandt.

"Pretty swanky." He stared at the two-story federalist-style house.

"His family has a lot of money. It added to his neurosis. Made him feel different, invincible, irresistible."

"He's going to need plenty of it for a good lawyer."

Two black-and-white units pulled into the circular driveway behind them.

Nick was already at the front door, gun drawn, waiting for his backup, when they climbed out of the car and took up a defensive position behind it.

Savannah moved closer to Kade, trying to make sense of the chills wiggling up and down her spine.

They were being watched.

She raised her gaze to a second-story window and saw a curtain drop back into place.

Three loud bangs preceded Nick Brandt's voice. "George Welte, open up! Montgomery police."

Nothing.

Savannah swallowed, trying to mentally smooth her tattered nerves. It would be over soon.

"We're coming in."

Detective Brandt reached out and pressed the door lever down. It opened and he entered the dark house, followed by a couple of uniformed officers.

Wayward flashlight beams glowed through the sheer curtains as the team cleared the lower level of the house.

Next to her she could feel Kade's barely contained restraint. He wanted to be inside.

"Did you see the curtains move upstairs?"

"What?" He looked over at her. "You saw someone upstairs?"

"No...I saw the curtains move and I felt like we were being watched."

"Probably Welte."

"Probably." She tried to relax, but couldn't. *Between Kade's nervous energy and the thought of what was transpiring inside, she couldn't think straight.*

"Cool it, will ya? They'll arrest him and we'll get a look around. Find the accelerant and incendiary devices linking him to the fires. He'll go to jail. End of story."

"End of story? What about us, Kade? Where does our story end?"

Mentally he froze, like a Popsicle in an icebox. She had to thaw him out, so she reached over and touched him, feeling her energy pulse into his body, melting away the igloo he'd encased his thoughts in.

It wasn't the right time to search for answers, but would there ever be a right time to ask the hard questions?

Where did they stand? Would they simply part company and vanish into the Montgomery landscape, leaving their connection an antiquated conduit neither one wanted to recharge? The thought made her sad.

The lights started coming on in the house, first upstairs, then down.

Nick Brandt stepped out onto the porch.

She knew something was wrong by the slump of his shoulders and the way he stood quietly for a moment before pulling his cell phone off his belt.

Kade must have sensed it, too, because he took her hand, giving it a squeeze. "We'll talk later."

They made it to the front steps as Nick dialed his cell phone, calling for a forensic team on scene.

"What's going on?" Kade asked.

Savannah's heart sank before Nick could give them the bad news. News she'd sensed the minute he'd come outside.

"We won't be talking to George Welte anytime soon." He closed his phone.

"He's dead."

Chapter Fourteen

The news forced the air out of Kade's lungs. It took him a moment to breathe again, but like waking from a bad dream, he could see the nitty-gritty details of the case vanish. He sobered.

"Hung himself in the upstairs bedroom."

"Suicide?" Kade asked, feeling a blade of regret slice into him.

"Looks that way. He must have come back here, knowing we were onto him. Poor bastard thought it was the only way out. It's too bad."

Kade squared his shoulders. "Yeah. And the information died with him, but you can't silence forensic evidence."

"We'll get the team in, then you can look around."

"Thanks." Kade stepped back as Nick moved past him to speak with a uniformed officer.

"I'm sorry, Savannah. I know you knew him. Maybe even liked him."

"He was odd, but nice…harmless…I thought, anyway."

He led her down the stairs and back to the car to wait until Watson arrived to prove what he already knew. There was an end in sight.

The fire spree was over, but he couldn't extinguish the slow burn sizzling in his body, welding him to her. It smoldered, threatening to explode into a firestorm and set him on fire if he gave it an ounce of oxygen.

KADE STARED at the cluttered workbench, a feeling of satisfaction in his soul. "We got him."

He glanced up, catching a brief look of doubt on her face, before he spoke. "It's all here. The incendiary devices, your purse, key ring. The muddy boots he was wearing when he abducted you. What more do you need?"

She'd shut him out, and try as he might, he couldn't get inside her head. "Look, here's the file he took from your office."

He picked up the file folder with George Welte printed in bold black letters and handed it to her.

She took it in her gloved hand and opened it, turning toward the single lightbulb that dangled from the attic ceiling. "You're right. It's all here. Neat and tidy." She read over the notes made in her own handwriting.

What further proof did she need? They'd landed in a gold mine, rich with all the nuggets they'd ever

need to tie George Welte to the fires, stalking, kidnapping. So why couldn't she concede?

She turned back toward him. "He was a pyro in
his teenage years, probably did it to get the attention
he craved from his distant parents. Later he got into
one obsessive relationship after another. He was
busted for being a peeping tom." She closed the file.
"It's classic."

Kade moved in next to her and folded his arms
around her. "In a perfect world, it would have been
caught early and fixed, but that's not what we live in."
He pulled in a breath, smelling the tang of citrus in
her hair.

His desire flared, hot…immediate.

He backed off and turned her loose. "They've
probably removed his body by now. Want to look
around the bedroom?"

"Yeah." She stepped past him and maneuvered
down the narrow stairway out of the attic.

He followed close behind her, weighing his emotions. She didn't need to be looked after anymore.
Welte was dead. Somehow, the thought of leaving her
alone didn't sit well in his gut, but there wasn't any
reason to continue taking up space in her guest room.
Besides, all he did was lay awake every night
wanting her.

Torture was officially over. He should be exuberant.

They ducked through the short, narrow door, and
stepped into the upstairs hallway.

"His room is there, on the left."

"What? I thought it was on the right. At least, that's where I saw the curtain…"

Savannah pulled in a deep breath. She didn't have the energy to argue the facts anymore. Even the nagging feeling in her gut was exhausted.

George Welte was their man. The evidence was overwhelming. What more did she need?

Don Watson was just coming out of the bedroom as they approached the doorway. "More stuff inside. He had it bad for you, Dr. Dawson."

"That's more information than I need."

"Sorry." Watson smiled sheepishly and padded down the stairs.

Her heart rate picked up as she followed Kade into the room, wondering what they'd find.

"Whoa!" Kade's response matched hers as she stared at a wall plastered with pictures of her.

"This is unbelievable. Look at this." She pointed out a snapshot of her with her hand in the flowerpot next to her front door. The one with the key tucked inside.

"I told you, your Pollyanna security system needed to be tightened up."

She glared at him, then stared at the picture next to it. "He followed me everywhere. The mall. The grocery store. My hairdresser. Every photo focused on some aspect of my life."

"He didn't like this."

She followed Kade's line of sight to a picture of

them together, huddled next to his car at a fire scene, but it was the big black X on Kade's face that spoke the loudest.

"Jealousy and obsession. It's a deadly combination."

She swallowed the lump in her throat. "You're right, of course. I just wish we could have talked to him. Dug into the reasons for all of this." She focused on the wall. "Jeez!" She shook her head, staring at the row of appointment cards from her office. "He must have kept every card he ever got."

Kade moved up to her elbow. "His obsession ran deep."

"I need some air." She backed away from the wall, wondering if she'd picked the right profession. She was supposed to help cure stuff like this, not get caught in the middle of it.

"Come on. I need to get you home."

"Okay." She stepped out of the room, but curiosity pulled her into the room across the hall. The room where she could swear she'd seen the curtains move and felt as if they were being watched.

"What is it?"

She looked around, finally staring up at the ceiling fan spinning on high speed. The wisps of air were strong enough she could feel them on her face. Strong enough to ripple the filmy drapes covering the window. She let go of the last of her doubt and closed the bedroom door.

"Okay. I'm satisfied. Let's go."

Kade smiled at her, shaking his head. "Good. Can I interest you in some breakfast?"

"Sounds wonderful." She followed him down the stairs and out into the early morning sunlight.

It seemed like an eternity since she'd relaxed. She wanted her life back, and now that was going to happen.

KADE MOVED along the corridor of the police station at a choppy pace, his cane tapping the floor, keeping time with his heart rate. The anticipation coursing in his veins bordered on the unreasonable.

It had been a week since George Welte had committed suicide, a long torturous week since he'd dropped Savannah off at her home and driven away with a knot in his gut and a hole the size of Texas in his chest.

"Kade." Nick reached out and shook his hand as he entered the briefing room. "Great job, buddy. I hear you're bucking for a promotion."

"Looks that way. With Jack Nelson retiring in a couple of years, they're looking to groom me for the position."

"All I can say is, you deserve it."

Kade glanced around the room, but didn't see Savannah. Disappointment stirred his emotions as he sat down. He wanted her to be here. Wanted her to know how much her input had helped the investigation…how much her touch had helped him.

"Sorry I'm late."

The sound of her voice supercharged him. He turned slightly, watching her come into the room, where she took a seat on his right.

"Glad you made it, doc." A smile spread on her lips, and his palms slicked. He tried to relax, to let her nearness soothe his agitated nerves. She was here, wasn't she? Sitting next to him. He couldn't ask for more.

"Let's get started." Police Chief Warren stood up. "As most of you know, we haven't had a fire in a week. Not since George Welte died."

A round of applause broke out.

"The department and the Arson Investigations office are satisfied we got our man. The lab has matched the chemical components of the cans of accelerant we obtained at his home to the components at the fire scenes. If you want details, visit with Kade." The chief nodded in his direction.

"Items focusing on Dr. Dawson were also recovered and support the belief that Welte was responsible for stalking her and for her abduction."

Kade's gut tightened. *He'd come as close as he ever wanted to get to losing her.* The air in the room thickened as he let the thought escape.

She must have caught it because she looked over at him, a knowing smile on her lips.

His desire bubbled to the surface and he fought to conceal it, tuning in on the chief's comments.

"The sole of the muddy boots we found in his house are a perfect match to the impressions taken at the scene of the doctor's abduction. Everyone did a fantastic job. Congratulations. There's going to be a small party at Sullivan's tonight."

A collective round of "Oh, yeahs" rumbled through the room.

"I'm picking up the tab. It starts at seven, hope to see you there." The chief stood up and walked around the table, a FedEx box in his hand. "This came for you."

Kade took the package, glancing at the return address. Chicago Fire Department. The case file was here. He put it on his paperwork stack. "Thanks, Chief."

"See you tonight?"

He glanced at Savannah. "We'll be there."

The chief left the room.

"Can I pick you up?" He studied her face, content just to stare at her, memorize her features, imprint the snapshot in his brain.

"Yeah. That would be great. I haven't had a night on the town for a while. I've heard of Sullivan's. Some sort of haunt for men in uniform?"

"Yeah. The best. My dad was at the opening in the early seventies. You'll like it. Six-thirty?"

"That works." She stood up.

The awkward moment set like cement in his mind, and he came up out of the chair. "Savannah?"

She stopped and turned toward him.

His nerves twisted around the words he wanted to say, and he almost let her go.

"I've missed you." He stared at her lips, wanting to feel them against his. Desire stirred his insides, pushing him forward, propelling him closer to the woman he wanted.

"I've missed you, too." Savannah reached inside his mind, intent on gathering his thoughts. The level of need she could feel in his body took her breath away and sent her pulse thumping out of control.

Gone was the selfish edge, his desire to touch her for pain relief alone. She released her resistance and he moved in close, so close she could smell the clean scent of his aftershave.

His body heat enveloped her as he clasped her shoulders in his hands.

The contact seared her, sending vibrations deep into her core. She wanted him. She wanted him in her life, in her bed, physically taking the liberties he was already exploring in his mind.

"My place? Tonight, after the party?" The choked suggestion was out before she could stop it. Heck, she didn't want to stop it. She wanted him. Wanted the fulfillment she knew only he could give her. The healing only she could give him.

"Are you sure?"

She stared into his dark eyes, glittering with unresolved emotion. Mentally, she traced his lips with her fingertip and heard him groan. She'd never been as sure of anything in her entire life.

THE SULTRY NOTES of a blues tune mixed with the tangle of voices in the restaurant half of the club.

Silverware clanked against plates. The air held the scent of grilled steak and buttery lobster, but Savannah could hardly look at the meal in front of her.

Since planning their hookup earlier in the day, she hadn't been able to think straight. Now, sitting across the table from Kade, she dared to look up and meet his smoldering gaze.

Liquid fire streamed through her body, coating her nerves in golden heat. The hunger in his eyes was hypnotic, and she fell into his trance, returning his vibe with the same fervor.

"Dance?" The request was barely out of his mouth when she pushed back her chair, taking his hand as he led her to the dance floor.

They mixed among the couples, moving to the slow rhythm of the song.

Kade folded Savannah in his arms, letting the contact infuse him with the life-sustaining energy he'd come to crave.

His pain evaporated like the clouds after a storm and he tightened his grip, memorizing her curves as he brushed his hands down her body, resting them on her narrow waist, feeling the sensuous movement of her hips in time with the music.

He closed his eyes for an instant, fighting the explosion in his body. It was sweet torture, he decided, as he moved her around the floor, lost in the connection welding them together. A connection he planned to fuse tonight in slow—

"Doctor Dawson?"

Savannah opened her eyes, not wanting to end the dreamlike reality she'd encased herself in, but she turned toward the man who'd addressed her.

It took her a moment to recognize Todd Coleman, her new tenant, with his arms around a tall blonde.

"I thought that was you. How are you?"

She felt Kade stiffen as she stopped moving and stepped back. "Great. Are you enjoying the house?"

"Yeah. It's just what I was looking for."

"Good." A shiver rippled over her skin and she stepped closer to Kade, convinced they were standing under an air-conditioning vent. That, or the internal fires they were stoking only gave off heat when they were locked together.

"Kade Decker, right?" Coleman extended his hand.

"Yes." Kade shook it. "I haven't seen you around much since you moved in."

"My job at the gas company keeps me pretty busy, and when I'm not working I like to come here." He indicated the club. "It keeps me up on the latest police and fire news, and I've gotten to know some of the guys."

"Sullivan's is the place for contacts." Kade glanced at Savannah, anxious to pull her back into his arms. "Have a nice one."

She didn't protest when he took her hand and twirled her around before pulling her back into his grasp.

He saw Coleman wink at the pretty blonde and move her into the sea of dancers.

He didn't like Coleman. Sure, he barely knew the guy, had only met him once, but he didn't like him or having to let go of Savannah while he made small talk.

"That's quite a coincidence."

"Yeah. He mentioned wanting to join the fire department, that day in front of your old house. I let it slide, but maybe he's really serious. He picked the right spot to get to know some of the troops."

"Yeah, yeah, yeah. All I want is for you to possess me again."

"Really." He stared down at her, and his world rocked. "Let's blow this place."

Savannah could only nod. She already had him undressed in her mind. Trailing kisses over his lips and down his broad chest.

He took her hand and led her over to the table where they said their thanks to the chief, but Nick Brandt stopped them just before they reached the door.

"The party's just getting started."

"I don't have much of an appetite tonight."

Nick stared from one to the other, a quirky smile spreading on his lips. "Enjoy your evening. You both deserve it." He popped Kade on the shoulder, and Savannah watched him move back to the table.

Over the crowd, she spotted Todd Coleman at the bar.

He saw her and raised his glass in a salute.

A shudder of anticipation raked over her skin and she tried to pick up on its source. There was excitement in the air, tension mixed with every other emotion possible. They flowed along with the people in the crowded club until she couldn't isolate a single person's vibes. She nodded to Coleman and turned with Kade to leave, aware of his eyes on them as they stepped out into the night.

KADE TRAILED his hand over Savannah's smooth skin, his blood turning to fire in his veins as the sensation flowed into his nerve endings and sizzled up his arm.

His muscles went taut, pulled tight with anticipation, need and myriad emotions he'd yet to explore.

Touching her was like completing a circuit. It drove deep shards of energy into his core. Healing energy that coursed through him, zapping his pain into oblivion as he wrapped his arms around her.

He was whole when he held her…alive when he let her in.

He unhooked the straps of her bra, pulled them

down and trailed kisses along the top of her right shoulder, sucking in the sweet vanilla scent on her skin.

His desire flared, glowing white-hot, burning his patience to a crisp. He popped the clasp on her bra and pulled it off, letting it fall onto the pile of discarded clothing at their feet.

A moan rumbled deep in her throat. He cupped her breast in his hand and brushed her nipple with his thumb until it peaked.

Shafts of half-light pushed through the slats in the blinds, illuminating the bedroom in dusky twilight. It was just enough light to see her body. To see the need on her face, in her eyes.

The last of his resistance crumbled as he picked her up in his arms and moved toward the bed, intent on catering to her wants, sating her desires along with his own.

Savannah pulled in a ragged breath and melted against Kade's chest.

The energy pulsating between them was growing more intense. Like nuclear fusion, it reacted out of control.

A tangle of hope and fear braided together inside her, leaving a knowledge she'd yet to accept.

Destiny had brought them together as children. Making love would join them, heal him, but...

She shoved her fingers into the hair at his nape, ignoring the irrational thought. She pulled in his smell, a layer of lime-tinged botanical, mixed with his own natural scent. She breathed him in until her heart and soul knew every nuance of the man she loved. But did he love her back?

He laid her down on the cool sheets, and she watched a slow sultry smile spread on his mouth.

Her heart pounded in her chest. All outside distraction fell away.

Reaching out, she touched his thigh and felt him resist, but he didn't pull away. His physical scars were evident, but she didn't find them ugly. They were simply a part of the man, like the color of his eyes or the shape of his mouth.

"Let go, Kade," she whispered, gazing into his eyes.

A moment of anguish crossed his handsome face. He clenched his teeth, resistance flexing the muscle along his jawline.

"These don't matter to me." She smoothed her hand over the healed burns that covered his thighs. Over the injury that had nearly killed him and locked his pain inside.

It's time to let go...time to heal...time to love.

He closed his eyes, and she knew he was fighting the battle. Fighting the recurring images that had directed and dictated his life for the past ten months, feelings of self-doubt, inadequacy and guilt. But she knew there was more inside of him. Courage, strength, determination. If only he'd accept them... let them fill the void.

He pulled her into his arms.

She arched against him, searching out his mouth with her own. Excitement pulsed in her body as she smoothed her hands over his chest, moving lower, taking pleasure in his reaction and silencing his groan with her lips as she teased him with her hand.

"Woman. Do you have any idea…"

"How long it's been?"

"How sweet it's going to be." He rolled her under him, growling as he pinned her arms over her head, their fingers interlocked. "You're so beautiful."

She stared into his dark eyes, smoldering with barely contained hunger. Her heart jolted in her chest. She closed her eyes, letting the compliment soak into her bones along with the pressure of his body molded to hers.

There would be a price to pay for what was about to happen between them; she knew it on a cosmic level. But a threshold had been crossed and she could never go back.

Kade released her hands, encircled her in his arms and rolled off her, taking her body with him. He was hot with need. Cocooned in an energy bubble, lost in the moment.

She stared down at him, a seductive smile on her perfect lips. His need flared and he cradled her face in his hands, pulling her mouth to his, tasting her kiss with his tongue. His body was on fire. Being consumed by an intense heat he couldn't understand, but refused to put out.

He ended the kiss and looked into her half-closed eyes. "Is this what you want?"

"More than the air in this room." She smiled and his desire skyrocketed as she spread her legs, opening for him.

A groan rumbled in his throat the instant he pushed into her, feeling her close around him. He sucked in a breath, rocking his hips, feeling the fire invade his body until he was ablaze, consumed by a vibration that came from the center of his soul.

Savannah moved against him, matching his rhythm. She could feel her life energy pass into his body, like it did every time they touched, but this time it was different.

There was no drain; instead, the contact energized her. She closed her eyes, riding the lightning wave of heat.

She was caught up in the frenzy that buzzed inside her head and encapsulated her body in indescribable pleasure.

She could feel the rhythm push her closer, closer to a mental and physical summit.

The buzzing inside her head turned to a hum. Showers of light rained behind her eyelids.

She reached orgasm, felt Kade's body tense as he followed her over the top and together they crashed into the light.

Spasms of pleasure squeezed her insides, shaking her to the core. A moan escaped her lips as she opened her eyes, staring down at him, at the smile of ecstasy on his mouth.

He moved several more times inside her, then slowed and stopped.

Savannah pushed off his chest and sat up, staring down at him. Whatever change she'd feared had taken place.

She'd known it the moment her body had gone white-hot and her brain had ceased to function for a moment. The exact instant he'd brought her to climax.

Kade opened his eyes and smiled up at her. Reaching out, he ran his hand along her cheek. His body felt weightless, a prisoner of some cosmic event he couldn't understand, but it didn't matter.

The smile of satisfaction on her lips said it all. Mentally, he searched for her thoughts. He'd come to enjoy playing around in her head, trying to catch her off guard, unprotected, vulnerable. But there was a layer he couldn't get through, a layer that hadn't been there before.

"Savannah?"

"What?"

"What am I thinking?" He grinned at her.

She closed her eyes, but opened them almost immediately. "I don't know anymore."

A stitch of concern dragged through him. He was

thinking how beautiful her eyes were. He'd mentally telegraphed the thought over and over.

He swallowed. "I was thinking about your eyes." He saw her smile fade and he knew. He knew what had just transpired between them had come at a price. Their ability to exchange thoughts was gone.

"It's over, isn't it?"

She moved off him, and he pulled her close.

"Yeah. I knew it the minute you set me on fire from the inside out." She raised up, resting her chin on her hands, tracing her finger over his hard muscled chest. "It was destiny's way of holding us together until our hearts met."

He stroked the hair off her cheek and considered her assessment. He'd felt the fire, all right; it had burned a path to his soul. Even the pain in his hip had been consumed, but a meeting of their hearts?

"Maybe you're right, Savannah."

A look of disappointment crossed her face and she lay her cheek against his chest. He stroked her hair, suddenly feeling alive in his own skin, something that hadn't happened in a long time.

He planted a kiss on the top of her head. "I'm going to shower. Wanna come?"

"No. Go ahead. This afterglow is wonderful. I'll be there in ten."

"Okay." He sat up, kissed her again and tucked the covers around her.

Savannah heard the bathroom door close and

snuggled into the pillow. Their mental connection was gone, but their physical connection had just come to life. It was an exchange she could live with.

The sound of water running lulled her into a half sleep and turned seconds into minutes, but the squeak of the bedroom door broke the moment.

Maybe Kade had forgotten something. Maybe he needed his razor from the shaving kit he'd left in the spare room.

A chill skittered over her skin, forcing her eyes wide open.

She listened, could still hear the shower running, but she knew she wasn't alone in the room.

In one short second, a hand slapped over her mouth.

She screamed into the sweaty palm, but the cry was muffled. Useless.

He yanked her out of bed.

She clutched the sheet around her naked body, pulling it off the bed as he slammed her against his chest.

"Let go," he whispered in her ear, his voice low and deadly.

Her blood turned cold in her veins. It was a voice she knew. The voice of her abductor. The voice of the man who'd come so close to killing her in the mud.

Fear sliced into her. She let go of the crumpled sheet, letting it drop to the floor.

Kade, she mentally screamed, but it was useless. Their bond was gone.

He snagged her robe off the bedpost. "Put this on."

She felt him reach into his front pocket, then watched as he threw a folded note onto the mattress.

"Hero freak," he hissed in her ear as he dragged her out of the bedroom and into the hallway.

He was strong, but she fought him anyway, scratched his arm, but he squeezed harder, pinching her in a choke hold.

She struggled to pull air into her lungs.

He paused at the front door and pulled it open.

Terror raced along her nerves, twisting up her spine, as he carried her into the night.

Chapter Fifteen

Kade let the hot water needle his skin and thought about Savannah. His new reality made him smile as he turned off the faucet.

He was in love with her.

It suddenly didn't matter that he wore scars on his body. It didn't matter what had gone before. There was only now. But would she have him? Was she willing to meld their lives together?

He snagged the towel off the bar and dried off. Already his body was wishing itself on her again.

He stalked out into the bedroom, his mind and body on fire, titillated by the details of making love to her again and again. But his desire crashed as he stared at the empty bed.

Caution worked through his system. It churned and settled in his gut as he walked over and flipped on the light switch.

The top sheet had been pulled from the bed, taking everything with it. Maybe she'd gone to the kitchen for something to eat. They'd both need sustenance to keep their strength up.

He smiled as he padded down the hall and stepped into the kitchen, but it was empty, too.

"Savannah?" he hollered, stepping into the living room.

Kade stopped, listening for a reply that never came. Worry sawed through him as he went to the front door.

It stood open a crack. He pulled the knob, opened the door, and stared out into the night.

Something was wrong. Dead wrong.

He charged down the hall and into the bedroom, pulling up short, his eyes locked on the folded piece of paper tossed on the bed.

It was too early for a Dear John letter.

He picked it up, unexplainable foreboding drumming in his mind. He opened the note and read the words scrawled in bold black letters. FOR SAM.

Kade's pulse hammered in his ears, his breathing escalated, but he couldn't get any oxygen. *Samantha Eldridge?*

Reality, cold and hard, sliced into his mind. He grabbed his clothes and pulled them on. There was only one way to be sure. One place he could find the answers, if only he'd have asked the right questions.

He bolted from the bedroom and went out to his car. Popping the trunk, he grabbed the FedEx package and raced back inside.

Tearing into the box, he pulled out the file Moynihan had sent him. Flipping it open, he studied the fire analysis from that night. The night he'd watched a young girl die. The night he'd wished to join her, prayed for the same reprieve from his torment.

"The incendiary device consisted of a cigarette, circled with stick matches and wrapped in paper, secured with a rubber band."

Horror laced through him and he looked up from the arson report. A report he'd been too damn damaged to look at. Too stunted to analyze with a distant perspective.

The Chicago arsonist and the Montgomery arsonist were one and the same. He choked back a guttural yell and scanned the balance of the report.

One name leaped out at him.

One name hammered in his brain. Todd Coleman.

Kade swallowed and reached for his phone, but the sound of the tones on his fire pager sent a shudder through him. .

"Engine Company 10, Company 14, Ladder Company 18, IC Fisk. Respond to a warehouse fire. 811 Monroe."

His breath caught. The final letter in the game. This fire on Monroe was for Sam. It had never been about Savannah, but she was the bait.

He bolted from the house, bent on destroying the man.

Todd Coleman had been Samantha Eldridge's boyfriend at the time of her death.

Todd Coleman, vanity arsonist, but there had never been enough evidence to implicate him in the fire that killed his girlfriend.

The blaze that had injured him and devoured ten months of his life.

Now he had Savannah.

Rage, poignant and explosive, squeezed his chest. He jumped into his car and took off for the scene, praying he got there in time.

In time to stop the flames from taking the woman he loved.

SAVANNAH PULLED IN one ragged breath after the next, cringing as Coleman wrapped another loop of duct tape around her ankles and pulled it tight, before moving up to secure her hands.

"Why are you doing this?"

A creepy smile split his lips, marring his features. "Because a hero freak chose to get in my way, and someone I loved died." He peeled a strip up on the roll and squeezed her wrists together.

"Kade?"

"Yeah. It was Decker that night. If he'd stayed out of my way, I'd have gotten to Sam, rescued her." A faraway look glazed his eyes, but it was tinged with madness.

She shuddered, trying to make sense of his obsession. "You killed George Welte."

"Stalking a stalker is easy. And his amateur fires,

set for you, were pathetic. Once I got his file from your office, I knew I'd found a fall guy."

"You stole my purse and keys that day in front of the rental?"

"Like taking candy from a baby, but George found me out. He was going to warn you. I couldn't let that happen. He would have ruined the finale, the blaze of glory you and your hero freak are going out in, so I killed him. Planted the evidence in the attic."

Terror jetted through her as she watched him reel off a four-inch piece of tape, just like in her premonition.

"I'm bait, aren't I? Just like Kade's mother was."

"Yeah." He smiled, a slow sick smile. "I wanted his attention, but the old bat survived. Then I saw the way he looked at you, touched you." He ran his finger down her arm.

Her stomach squeezed. "And the snakes in the pool?"

"Just a little surprise to make things more interesting, but he'll come. The bastard will come and there won't be any help for either of you tonight. Now lie down and shut up." He slapped the strip of tape over her mouth and smoothed it with his hand.

He stood up, and nudged her with his booted foot until she went horizontal against the cement floor of the warehouse. A massive framed catacomb of rooms and hallways, a maze of death.

Savannah swallowed the fear rocking her soul.

Todd Coleman had been stalking all of them for weeks.

Watching…waiting…burning for revenge.

She trailed her gaze around the room, focusing on a narrow piece of metal gas line circling the perimeter.

He planned to cook her…alive.

The gruesome nature of the crime made her stomach lurch as she watched him put on fire gear, a turnout coat and bunker pants. He slapped on a fireman's helmet and picked up a fire ax.

The weapon from her premonition. She had to come up with a plan. Some way to warn Kade.

Coleman left the room.

Jerking against her bonds, she tried to loosen the tape, but it was useless. It might as well be steel.

The hiss of gas entered her ears and terrorized her mind as the sickeningly sweet smell set her nerves on edge.

The final horror came to life as the gas ignited and three foot high flames shot out of the ports in the pipe.

An inferno, hot and deadly, surrounded her, a wall of fire superheating the room.

She pulled in a breath and closed her eyes, the details of her nightmare becoming reality. There was only one player missing.

KADE SLAMMED ON the brakes, killed the engine and jumped out of the car. In the distance he could hear the wail of sirens, but they were ten minutes out.

He popped the trunk, staring at his father's old fire gear. He'd stashed it in the trunk of his car after hearing Savannah's premonition of his death. After finally trusting her.

Shreds of her nightmare whirled in his mind. He pulled out the details he remembered. Details that could save his life or end it.

His heart slammed against his ribs as he donned the gear, grabbed a spare air tank, and turned toward the warehouse.

An eerie glow radiated from the bowels of the building, flickering through the skylights in the roof. An unearthly warning that sliced into his psyche and challenged him to move forward.

He glanced at the sky for signs of smoke, but there weren't any. Caution hedged his advance. Savannah was inside, he knew it, could feel it in his bones, but what the hell kind of game was Coleman playing?

It didn't matter, he decided as he slipped into the darkness, bent on having her again. The moment of truth had come. He'd face his demons, now, tonight, or die trying.

SAVANNAH WATCHED in horror as the flames steadily grew higher, licking the ceiling and creating burn spots on the tiles.

Every passing second was turning Coleman's controlled burn into an out-of-control inferno, making escape less of a reality.

She'd lost track of Todd Coleman, but it didn't matter. Her survival instincts kicked in.

She rolled over, closer to the flames. Closer to the only thing that could free her, but four feet from the wall she had to stop. The heat was too intense. So hot she could almost feel her skin melting.

She pushed back. There had to be a way to get her arms free. She scanned the fiery room, but it was bare. Nothing that could help her. She sat up, pulled her legs underneath her and rocked onto her knees. Putting her hands on the floor to stabilize herself she tried to stand up, but Coleman had crossed her ankles. She wobbled and fell backwards onto her butt.

Trying again, she struggled toward the doorway, but the heat was too intense. She pulled back.

Staring at the doorway, she saw movement.

She sucked in a breath as watery tears blurred her vision.

Kade? She blinked them away, panic in her heart and visions of the death premonition in her head. But it was Coleman, setting up for the kill.

KADE SLIPPED into the warehouse, scanning for any signs of Savannah or Coleman. Nothing.

The air was laced with the odor of lighter fluid, but he couldn't draw a bead on where the smell was coming from. He moved deeper into the building. The abandoned warehouse had been divided by a series of huge wooden partitions, dissecting it into a maze. He certainly felt like a rat, attempting to work his way through them, searching for the prize.

Kade stopped, listening to the sounds inside the structure. Hoping for an indication he was on the right track.

It came, fast and hot, as a flash fire ignited in the corridor, bursting from a pile of rags. Coleman's MO. How many more of the deadly devices had he planted?

Kade lunged forward and around the flames, aiming for the center of the building. The spot where he could see fire reflecting against the ceiling overhead.

Another fire hissed to life, somewhere in the building, then another, but he kept moving forward even as the air began to blacken with smoke.

He felt the heat intensify and broke into a run.

She didn't have much time left. Fear knifed into his heart, pushing him forward, through the flames, now beginning to consume the walls of the box they'd been shut in.

Visions of that night ten months earlier flared inside his mind, begging him to retreat, but he pushed forward. He wouldn't lose her. He couldn't lose her.

Kade reached the core of the building and paused. He raised his arm against the heat and stared through the circle of flames.

His heart pounded out of control, his nerves twisted into knots.

Then he saw her, sitting in the middle of the floor, unmoving.

"Savannah!"

She startled and stared at him through the fire, terror in her ice blue eyes.

He had to get to her, had to charge the flames.

A noise to his right caught his attention. He turned in slow motion, staring up at the fire ax raised above his head.

Savannah's warning drummed in his mind. He reacted, pulling backward half a step.

The ax whooshed past, inches from his face, and sliced into his right thigh.

Bright red blood pulsed from the slash. He felt it run down his leg and pool in his boot.

Searing pain cut into his body and for an instant his mind went numb, but he stared at Savannah in the midst of the fire, her eyes wide with panic and he raged forward, whirling toward his attacker.

Coleman raised the ax, ready to send another blow crashing down on him.

Kade charged forward, tackling him.

The force sent Coleman backward, slamming him against the wall.

His eyes widened behind the face shield as he slid down the wall in slow motion, a trail of blood on the wall behind him.

The tip of the ax handle stuck up over his right shoulder.

Horror rushed his mind. There was nothing he could do for Todd Coleman, but he had to save Savannah.

He rolled Coleman over and pulled the fire ax out of his back, dropping the bloodstained weapon on the floor. His stomach turned as he pulled the bloody turnout coat off of Coleman's lifeless body.

He stumbled forward, his head spinning. The blood loss from his leg was dragging him closer to unconsciousness.

Determination pulsed in his veins as he fought for his life and hers.

Todd Coleman's staged fire began to ignite the ceiling.

Kade spotted the propane tank on the other side of the room and choked down his terror. The tank could explode at any time. They wouldn't stand a chance in hell of getting out if he didn't shut off the gas.

Pushing forward he hugged the wall—now smoldering, ready to flash—and reached the tank. Turning the valve, he shut off the gas.

The fire hissed and blew out.

He rushed to her.

Ripping the duct tape from her ankles, he freed her legs, then her hands and finally pulled the tape from her mouth.

The fire raged and popped around them, igniting the last of Kade's strength. "Put this on!" He helped her into Coleman's turnout coat, put the self-contained breathing apparatus on her back and positioned the mask on her face.

He grabbed her hand.

"Run!" They raced toward the entryway and escape.

His heart pounded in his chest, his lungs screamed for oxygen.

Fire, angry and red, burned the interior of the warehouse, consuming everything in its path.

He never let go of her hand, just stayed focused on the exit. In one final push, he pulled her through the doorway and out of the inferno.

The scream of sirens filled the night air as Kade led Savannah a safe distance away.

He'd done it. He'd saved the woman he loved. He was whole again. He'd challenged the flames and won.

His heart raced in his chest, his eardrums pounding with the echo of his pulse.

He could feel his life draining away. Running out of the gash on his thigh. It was a mortal wound. He'd known it the instant Coleman had sliced into his femoral artery.

He collapsed on the ground, staring up at Savannah as she knelt next to him on the hard Alabama earth.

"I love you," he whispered, and his world crashed.

"KADE! KADE!" Panic laced around Savannah's mind as she bent over Kade's still body.

"No! No you don't. You can't die on me, I won't let you."

She stared at his thigh, at the amount of blood pulsing out of the wound. She wouldn't live without him.

She had to get it stopped.

Untying the belt on her robe, she pulled it off. He could lose his leg, but it was the only way to save his life.

She wrapped the belt around his upper thigh and pulled it tight, tying it in a knot. Feeling around on the ground, she found a thick stick and shoved it in between his leg and the belt.

Turning it slowly she wound the tourniquet tight, as she watched a paramedic unit roll up on the scene, followed by a string of fire engines.

KADE'S MIND was awake, even if his body wasn't.

He listened for familiar sounds, trying to get his bearings.

Was he still alive? Or was he hanging in the afterlife?

And where was Savannah? He'd gotten her out of the burning warehouse, stolen her from inside Coleman's inferno. If this was heaven, they'd let him in.

A constant blip registered in his mind at the same time he realized he could feel his arms and legs. Just to be sure he wiggled his feet, first the left, then the right.

"Kade?"

Her voice filtered through to his mind, setting his hopes on fire.

He worked to open his eyes, worked to pull himself back into the land of the conscious.

Her hand smoothed against his cheek. He could hear the subtle whispers of her grief. Was she crying?

"Come back to me, Kade. Please come back."

He opened his eyes, staring up at her.

The face of his fire angel.

Savannah swallowed. Tears of joy clouded her vision and squeezed her throat shut. "I always knew you were a fighter."

He reached up, trapping her hand against his cheek, feeling her brand of intoxication invade his body, making him drunk with need.

"What did you do back there?"

"A tourniquet, and I was your transfusion donor when they got you to the hospital. It seems we're the same type."

"That explains why I feel you in my blood." He studied her face and watched her smile fade.

She was in his blood literally, but she was lodged somewhere else as well. Somewhere sacred and forever.

"I love you, doc." He kissed her fingers, one by one. "I'm never going to let you go. Will you stay, start a fire with me?"

Savannah's heart expanded in her chest. "It's destiny. It started twenty-eight years ago." She watched an easy smile spread on his lips and bent over him, kissing him until desire flared in her veins.

She pulled back just as Nick Brandt appeared in the doorway and walked into the room.

"Well, looks like you made it, Decker, and you get the girl."

Kade snorted and flashed his buddy a grin. "I do, don't I?"

"You're a lucky sucker."

"Yeah." He smiled at Savannah and pressed the controls on his bed to raise his head.

"Any chance Coleman survived?"

"No. Savannah told us what happened. Seems his backswing was a real killer."

Kade sobered, realizing how close they'd come to dying and how quickly life could end. "I take it you got hold of Mac Moynihan's report?"

"Yes. Seems Todd Coleman had it in for you ever since you rescued his girlfriend, Samantha Eldridge."

Kade swallowed. "Correction. Tried to rescue her. She died in the fire. It must have set him off, turned him from a vanity arsonist to a revenge arsonist."

"We found a copy of George Welte's file in the bedroom at Savannah's rental on Palm Street. I suspect he stole the original, read up on Welte's psychosis and then planted it at Welte's place along with all the evidence. There was also a batch of incendiary devices that tie him to the major fires."

"He stalked Welte, while Welte was stalking me. George was setting some of the blazes, so Coleman set him up to take the fall for everything. I don't think he planned on dying in that warehouse."

Kade reached out and squeezed Savannah's hand, feeling her energy flow into him and reversing the floodgate. "It's over now."

Nick Brandt turned toward the door. "I'm out of here. I'll leave you two alone. Let me know when you bust out. We'll get together for dinner."

"Thanks, buddy." Kade leaned back against the pillow and trained his eyes on Savannah.

"Come here." He patted the edge of the bed, satisfied when she sat down next to him. "Since destiny has already interfered, maybe we should give in. What do you say?"

Her heart jumped in her chest. "I say yes, but can you live with a wacko like me, picking up on your emotions 24/7?"

"I can't live any other way." He pulled her into his arms.

She basked in the feel of him, in the thought of sharing their lives, forever melded by the fire that had joined them since childhood.

"I love you, Kade, but you have to promise you'll stay out of burning buildings."

"Trying to change me already?"

"Without the proper equipment," she added.

"Deal."